1. Get gorgeous hair

I shampooed my hair. The only problem was that though the water made the false hair go completely fuzzy and wrinkled, not much of it actually came off. And when I tried to dry it with the hair dryer there was a terrible smell of burning, and smoke started to come out of it.

"This is getting even worse!" I wailed.

I noticed that Anna didn't disagree with me. She was about to say something when there was a knock on the door and her mum came in.

"Oh my God!" She put her hand up to her mouth. "What on earth have you two been doing?"

Also available from Simon Pulse

Ella Mental

Love & Sk8

Mates, Dates, and Inflatable Bras

A Novel Idea

The Princess & the Pauper

10
Things
to Do
Before
You're
16

Caroline Plaisted

SIMON PULSE

New York   London   Toronto   Sydney

SIMON PULSE
An imprint of Simon & Schuster Children's Publishing Division
1230 Avenue of the Americas, New York, NY 10020
Copyright © 2005 by Caroline Plaisted
Originally published in Great Britain in 2005 by Simon & Schuster UK
Published by arrangement with Simon & Schuster UK
First U.S. edition 2006
All rights reserved, including the right of reproduction in whole or in part in any form.
SIMON PULSE and colophon are registered trademarks of Simon & Schuster, Inc.
Designed by Paula Russell Szafranski
The text of this book was set in Granjon.
Manufactured in the United States of America
First Simon Pulse edition June 2006
10 9 8 7 6 5 4 3
Library of Congress Control Number 2005935011
ISBN: 978-1-4424-1422-8

Chapter One

"How can I have got to be so old and still be so boring?" I wailed. It was a Saturday night. My fifteenth birthday, no less. And was I out clubbing with my mates wearing the latest Miss Sixty jeans?

As if!

Instead, I was stuck with my best friend Anna in my bedroom, listening to a live concert via the Internet.

No boys. No designer labels. Just me and Anna. Having a sleepover. Exactly the same as my fourteenth birthday . . .

"I bet *Frankie* isn't stuck inside on a Saturday," Anna said.

Frankie Martinetti is the most amazing girl at

school. She's dead glamorous, with long legs and shiny hair, and it's simply inconceivable that she doesn't go out clubbing every Saturday night. In fact, she's the sort of girl that gets let in free by the bouncers. I know so—because she's told everyone at school about it.

Oh yes—that's the other thing about Frankie: She's a right pain. And she has an extremely large head, on account of the fact that all the boys in school fancy her something rotten.

"Right," I said to Anna, throwing myself back against the pillow on my bed in disgust. "And I bet Frankie's parents don't say she's too young to go out with her friends on their own for *her* birthday."

You see, Anna and me'd had this great idea for celebrating my birthday by going to Cheeky Pete's, the new club in town. Even though it was Over 18s only, Frankie had already been there with Trish, Vic, and Sylvie (affectionately—NOT!—known to me and Anna as the Frankie-ettes). And they'd made sure that everyone at school knew about it.

Oh boy, did they! How easy it was for them to get in because they looked so sophisticated and cool. How fit the talent was. How each of them had met some older lad. How they'd all got a lift back in an open-top car. And how they'd all been invited out for other dates afterwards.

It just wasn't fair!

So, for my fifteenth birthday, I'd got this plan with

Anna to tell my mum and dad that we were off to the multiplex to see a film and have a pizza. But instead, natch, we were going to go to Cheeky Pete's. Simple.

And then Mum had said: "What a great idea, Beth! We'll book the tickets in advance. What film would you like to see?"

I was like—"*What?* You think me and Anna want to be seen out with you, Dad, and my baby brother?" *Especially when we want to be giving it some down at Cheeky Pete's?*

And then my dad had said: "Don't talk to your mother like that!"

And I am so pathetic and useless that instead of going to Cheeky Pete's for my birthday, Anna and I ended up down at the multiplex with my mum, dad, and baby brother. At least the pizza afterward was okay. But it wasn't exactly cool, was it?

Back in my bedroom afterward, Anna and I listened to an Internet gig and despaired.

"We've got to do something about this," Anna said.

"About what?"

"Stuff," Anna mumbled, through the gum she was chewing. "If my life carries on being as dull as this, I think I'm going to die."

"Oh, right. Chuck us that magazine, will you?" I replied. If I couldn't be out being cool, at least I could read about other people out being cool.

I flicked through the pages. But I'd read the magazine twice already, so it didn't have anything new in it that was going to take me by surprise. Or at least I didn't think so, until I got to the page with the reader makeover on it. There was a frumpy girl with quite disgusting clothes in the "before" picture. After dyeing her hair, burning her outfit, and taking her to Top Shop, the "after" picture showed someone who was funky and sassy.

"That's it!" I said, throwing the article at Anna. "That's what we've got to do!"

"What?" Anna said, looking at it. "Dribble some paint down the front of our trousers? That'll *really* go down well with our parents. Not!"

"No—you don't get it!" I said, sitting up. "Don't you see? Everyone else at school is doing cool stuff and we're the only ones who are missing out!"

"Oh—like I hadn't noticed?" Anna sighed, chucking the magazine on the floor and snuggling back down inside her sleeping bag.

"Look!" I spluttered impatiently. "In exactly twelve months' time, we're going to be sixteen, aren't we?"

"Well—eleven months for me, actually," Anna pointed out. She'd had her birthday party last month in her parents' new conservatory (Her gran was there! Please!).

"Whatever," I said. "The point is, we've got twelve months before we're sixteen. You can leave school and get a proper job at sixteen if you want to!"

"Meaning?" Anna said. I could tell she was beginning to get interested in what I was saying because she started to sit up.

"Meaning, it's up to us to do something about it," I said.

"About what?" Anna asked.

"About our lives being so boring!" I exclaimed. "It's all in those magazines, isn't it?"

Anna looked at me without saying anything.

"You know," I urged. "All these other girls are doing loads of stuff that we're missing out on!"

"Like boys and clubbing," Anna agreed.

"And decent clothes and great hair—loads of other stuff!" I urged.

"There's no need to rub it in," Anna sighed, patting her blonde frizz. "So what are we going to do about it?"

"Make a list!" I said, leaping out of my bed and trying to find a piece of paper and a pen from the pit that was meant to be my desk.

"Of the stuff we haven't done?" Anna asked.

"Yes!" I said. "And all the stuff that we need to do!"

"Things we should have done by the time we're sixteen." Anna smiled. "*Now* I get it!"

"Exactly!" I grinned. "Right—what should be number one?"

A few minutes later, I was sitting there with a piece of paper—Groovy Chick because my mum still thinks that's cool for someone who is fifteen—and my pen poised.

"Number one is hair, right?" I asked Anna.

"Definitely," she declared.

"What *about* our hair? Cut it? Grow it?"

"Grow it, of course! Kind of Beyoncé style. Think long, luscious, shiny, thick . . ." As she said it, Anna gestured round her head with her hands.

"Hey, do you think we could?" I wondered, running a strand of my boring brown hair through my fingers.

"We've got a year, haven't we? We can have some hair treatments too," Anna said confidently.

"Minor problem," I said. "Hair treatments cost loads. And we ain't got no cash."

"Don't be so pathetic," said Anna. "We haven't even started yet. We can get a book out of the library on how to do them ourselves. I'm sure I read somewhere that you can use cheap stuff like eggs and cooking oil to make your hair shiny."

"Seriously?" I asked suspiciously.

"Just write it down, Beth! Here—give me the list." Anna grabbed it from me and scribbled on the paper. "So, what's number two?"

"Hmm." I thought hard. "There's so much we're missing out on it's—it's hard to work out what *shouldn't* be on the list! But I know I'd like to look like Christina Aguilera in a pair of jeans."

"Or Britney," said Anna. "Yes! That's a must!" She wrote it down with a flourish.

"Are we really going to go for it?" I asked.

"Like, hello? Does Robbie Williams have gorgeous eyes?" Anna said, her head on one side.

I laughed. "Okay—how about learning to walk in really high heels?"

"Really *really* high heels! Number three!"

This was beginning to be fun. At last, my birthday was picking up.

Chapter Two

Now, fast forward nine months. Don't get me wrong. We are not so sad that we are still working out the ten things that should be on our list. No way! A few things changed, but we got ourselves a list all right and it was good. We started on it straight away. We were growing our hair from the word go.

So by now we should look super cool, right? Er, well . . . Actually, we look exactly like we did a year ago. Only with hair that is a bit longer.

Okay, I admit it, we didn't exactly get on with our list once we finished it. I was kind of cross with myself about that. I mean, I'm going to be sixteen in only three months' time and I'm still not the fab glam über-babe I was hoping to be. Nowhere near . . .

@

It was a Sunday afternoon. A boring Sunday afternoon. The type where your parents have fallen asleep on the sofa in the living room, having made a huge fuss about you not being allowed to switch on the telly 'at this hour' because you should be Enriching Your Knowledge by reading the newspapers. I mean, please—my dad was fast asleep with the newspaper over his face and my mum was just asleep. And they were BOTH snoring.

Will—he's my obnoxious younger brother—had commandeered the telly to use the Play Station. So I'd taken refuge in my bedroom. I lay on my bed for a while, wondering when exactly things were going to get a bit more interesting. That's when I started thinking about my last birthday and the famous list that Anna and I had come up with. I'd originally put it in my wardrobe so that every time I opened the door it was there in front of me. But I hadn't seen it for a while. It must have fallen off. I just couldn't face another pizza-and-movies birthday. If I did, it would mean that nothing had changed in my life since I was fourteen! So I got up and opened the wardrobe. The list was scrumpled up on the floor in a corner. I smoothed it out. Anna and I had spent ages working out what the final ten things should be. It had gone through several drafts, but this was what we'd ended up with:

Ten Things Anna and Beth Are Going to Do Before They're Sixteen

1. Get gorgeous hair
2. Anna: Get ears pierced
   Beth: Get a tattoo
3. Get and wear a pair of super-high stilettos (without falling over)
4. Go out with the two school hotties—Baz and Greg
5. Get a job and earn loads of dosh
6. Get into a club
7. Get perfectly tanned, fuzz-free legs
8. Get a Wonderbra
9. Have fantastic nails
10. Be dead cool and sophisticated

It had all seemed such a good idea nine months ago. And, to be honest, with my sixteenth birthday fast approaching, it still seemed quite a good idea now. Actually, a *very* good idea. So I grabbed my mobile and gave Anna a call.

"Oh God, Beth!" Anna wailed down the phone.

"Do you have to ring me on what is probably the most boring day of the week just to remind me how boring I am?"

"Give me a break, Anna! I'm just pointing out that we've still got a little bit of time to do the stuff on this list," I said.

"What list? Oh . . . *that* list. But I thought we were meant to do all that *before* we were sixteen, remember? And I'm sixteen in a couple of months' time!"

"I know," I sighed, feeling guilty.

"Still," Anna added, "I suppose we *could* have another look at it . . ."

"You're up for it?" I said, cheering up immediately.

"Your place or mine?" Anna said. "My brother's here with a load of mates, watching footie."

"No question, then," I giggled. I knew Anna wouldn't want to be around a bunch of boys watching footie with, I'm sure, their trainers off and their disgusting smelly feet on display. "See you here in ten!"

Fortunately, Anna doesn't live that far away—so she was round and in my bedroom almost before I'd had time to boil the kettle. I made us each a cup of coffee while she got comfortable.

She was flopped down on my bed when I came back in with the drinks.

"I see you've got the list out," Anna said, picking it

up from my duvet. "Snap!" She pulled her copy from the pocket of her jacket. "I've been keeping it in my diary," she explained.

"So where should we begin? We've kind of already started on the hair thing, haven't we?" I said hopefully.

"Well," Anna said thoughtfully. "It *is* longer but I'm sure we could do something better with it. I mean, *look* . . ."

She pulled at the curly blonde strands that framed her face, then ruffled her hair over her eyes. "Not exactly Beyoncé, is it?"

I had to agree. And my shapeless brown mop was even worse. "Well, we could do those hair treatments, couldn't we? That stuff you read about olive oil and egg whites?"

"Okay," Anna said, sitting up and looking a lot more enthusiastic than when she'd first arrived. "And we could get it styled too. Lots of hairdressers have student nights—we could go to one of those. So, what's next on the list . . . ?" She read down the page. "Getting my ears pierced—no probs. Aha—you need a tattoo!"

I gulped. "Yeah."

A tattoo. It had seemed a good idea nine months ago. I've already had my ears pierced so there was no point in doing that again. But a tattoo. Suddenly it sounded kind of painful.

But before I could think any more about it, Anna was on to the list again.

"Shoes!" she said, slapping the list down on the bed.

"Oh yeah—the stilettos," I replied. "They've got some to die for at Sole Mate in town."

"Course they have," Anna said. "All the shoes in that shop are to die for. And somebody would have to die and leave us loads of money before we could afford them."

"Your point being?" I said grumpily.

"My point is, we have to source our stilettos from somewhere cheaper," Anna said firmly.

"Like where?" I wondered out loud. "I don't know about yours, but my mum doesn't exactly make a style statement in the shoe department. Stilettos are definitely not on her list of 'comfortable shoes.' So we won't be able to raid *her* wardrobe."

"Boot fair," Anna said smugly.

"Where's Boot Fair?" I asked. "Never heard of it."

"*A* boot fair," Anna said. "*The* car boot fair at the station. I bet that woman who always has those great clothes will have some stilettos!"

"Oh yes!"

Anna was right. We'd been to the boot fair a couple of times to find stuff to wear to the school disco. There was this crazy woman who was always there, with amazing wild hair and an equally amazing collection of clothes and jewelery. I couldn't remember spotting any shoes but it did seem reasonable to expect that she would have some in her stall.

"So, shall we go there next week?" I asked.

"What's the time?" Anna demanded. Anna has this thing about watches. She reckons it's completely uncool to wear one. Consequently she is late for everything. Which I don't think is that cool. At least when she's supposed to be meeting *me*. But it doesn't seem to bother Anna.

I glanced at my watch. "Three o'clock," I said. "Why—do you have to go home already?"

"No." Anna leaped up and grabbed her coat. "Come on! There's still time to catch her."

"Catch who?" I said, grabbing my own coat from behind the bedroom door.

"The clothes lady at the boot fair!"

Of course Anna was right. Not only was the amazing clothes lady there, but she did indeed have a selection of shoes. Some were quite disgusting: horrible Seventies platforms and nasty plastic Sixties boots. But Anna pounced on a couple of pairs of stilettos in a box.

One of the pairs was staggeringly high, with toe-pinchingly sharp points. Everything we needed—except that they were white.

"There is NO WAY I will be seen dead in a pair of white stilettos!" I cried.

"We could dye them!" Anna suggested, refusing to be defeated as she struggled to get them on. "They're too small for me. Do they fit you?"

She started trying on the other pair, which were plain black—although they did have diamanté down the heel. I wasn't sure which was worse.

The white shoes fit me—though they didn't look so good with my socks on.

"Hey—these fit me!" said Anna triumphantly, squeezing her feet into the black pair like a regular ugly sister. "How much for both?"

They were two pounds each pair and a deal was struck.

"Now all we've got to do—," said Anna, as we ambled back to her house, wearing our trainers again, "—is practice walking in them so we look like Sarah Jessica Parker!"

Chapter Three

"Who do you think they belonged to before?" I asked as we walked back to Anna's. "I mean—do you think they're, you know . . . clean?"

"Clean?" Anna spluttered. "Of course they're clean."

"But—you know, verrucas. They might have stuff like that on them, mightn't they?"

"*Eurgh*. I hadn't thought of that. Gross!" Anna wrinkled her nose. She went quiet for a moment, then linked her arm through mine. "Tell you what, we'll wipe them out with some bleach when we get back to mine. That should sort it."

So we did. We sneaked the bleach up to Anna's bedroom and smeared some inside each shoe. It made them smell quite disgusting, but at least it would get rid of any foot fungi that might be lurking.

"Well, no one can accuse us of having smelly feet now!" I said, slipping the shoes on. "Ooo-er!" An extra four inches of heel when you're used to walking round in trainers is quite a lot. Suddenly the ceiling seemed much closer. An extra four inches of heel is also quite, well, *wobbly*.

"How does Sarah Jessica manage to run in these things?" I marveled, as I tottered across Anna's bedroom.

Okay, so our mums would kill us if they knew, but we always watched the *Sex and the City* reruns after we were supposed to have gone to bed. And all the women on that show wear unbelievably high heels and still manage to run for taxis without so much as an ankle twitch, let alone actually falling down.

"Practice," Anna said, slipping on her shoes and joining me in my amble. "I read about it in *Cosmo Girl*. Sarah Jessica practiced, just like we are now, so that in the end she was able to run in her Manolos."

After a few minutes, the shoes did begin to feel a bit more normal. And being so high did make me feel kind of powerful—if a little shaky.

"Hey—I could get used to these," I said, flicking my hair out of my eyes and looking at myself in the mirror.

17

"Anna?"

There was a knock on the door but before Anna could say anything, the door was shoved open and her older brother Joey burst in.

"Do you want some—Oh!"

Joey stopped and stared. "What are you doing?" He looked at our feet. And then he started to laugh. *Really* laugh.

I'd known Joey for as long as I'd known Anna. Once upon a time, he'd been someone it was okay to kick a football around with. Then he'd gone through a geeky stage and we'd kind of ignored him. Now he was nearly six feet tall, with this very white blond hair. He was seriously into sports and dead fit. In both senses of the word. Which, for some reason, made me feel embarrassed these days. And I felt especially embarrassed standing there in my heels, like a kid playing dress-up.

"Oh, Joey, give it a rest," Anna said, scrambling to get her stilettos off.

Suddenly, the heady feeling of power I'd had only a few minutes ago disappeared and a feeling of complete stupidity overwhelmed me. I sat down on Anna's bed and took my shoes off. I felt like an idiot.

An idiot who, to my horror, now had bright red feet that were stinging and itching. And the more I itched, the more they stung. So much for the brilliant idea of putting bleach in our shoes . . .

◎

"That was just so awful!" I whined to Anna the next day on our way to school. I could feel myself blushing at the thought of how ridiculous I must have looked to Joey.

"Not good, I admit," Anna said. "But hey—Joey is always taking the piss out of me. You kind of get used to it after a while."

We walked along in silence for a while and then I said, "So do you think we could dye my shoes black like yours?"

"No probs," Anna said. "We'll get some dye at lunchtime."

"I wish we could have just gone and bought a decent pair of shoes in the first place," I moaned. "I've got to get my hands on some money!"

"Too right," Anna confirmed. "What we need are some jobs!"

In the classroom the next day, waiting for registration, Frankie was holding court. She's been in our class ever since we started school, and for some bizarre reason—other than the fact that she's stunning-looking—everyone loves her. The teachers, the students, well, the Frankie-ettes anyway. They worship her and every word she utters. Some girls in my class are desperate to be in her group of friends. Not us, of course. No way.

Well . . . we did want to be part of her crowd *once*. But lately, we've got kind of tired of Frankie—and her friends, who spend all their time sucking up to her and telling her just how fab she is.

On this particular morning, Frankie was telling everyone about her weekend. Apparently, she'd been shopping at Top Shop in central London with a friend when she'd been approached by someone from a model agency.

"She said I had this, like, totally different look," Frankie boasted, lounging across the desk. "And she's asked me to come and see her at her agency. She's given me her card."

Frankie kind of purred as she said it.

"The cat's got the cream," Anna hissed under her breath.

I nudged her with my elbow. I knew what she meant, but it would be awful if Frankie heard.

"Isn't that amazing?" Sylvie sighed, as if the Frankie glow had spread to her, too.

Most of the other girls in the class nodded and muttered their agreement. Anna and I just scowled.

"Do you really think it's true?" Anna said on our way home that afternoon. Frankie and her cronies had gone on and on about the model agency stuff all day. It was enough to make you puke.

"Probably," I muttered. "And she'll probably get a

million pounds for her first shoot, a gorgeous rock star will fall in love with her, and her face will be on every bus in London. But hey, who cares?"

Anna laughed. "Talking about a million pounds," she said, "what are we going to do about earning some money ourselves?"

"We could see if there are still some jobs going at the Outlet," I suggested.

The Outlet was this huge shopping center just outside of town. It had opened a few months earlier and had loads of designer shops that were selling off last season's stock. Frankie worked there sometimes.

"Listen, it's bad enough spending all week listening to Frankie drone on—I do *not* want to be in the same place as her on Saturdays as well!"

"Agreed!" I laughed. "So—what about the shops in town?"

"Good idea," Anna agreed. "Let's wander down the High Street now and see what we can find."

Chapter Four

We went into the chemist's first. It was no good.

"Sorry—we have a waiting list for jobs here," said a rather snooty woman with a badge saying "Line Manager." I mean, please: Does anyone need to manage a line?

The man in the supermarket said yes, he had jobs. We thought things were looking up until he explained that it meant working from 7:30–10:30 p.m. every Friday and Saturday night, restacking shelves after the shop had shut. Bye bye, social life . . . er no, make that bye bye, Mr. Supermarket.

"Pants," I moaned to Anna as we left the store.

"Nah—who wants to work in a supermarket wearing an overall anyway?" Anna said.

Next stop was the library but there was nothing doing there either. We got the same response from all the clothes shops too, though a couple of them said that they'd take our details and call us if vacancies came up.

We ended up at the Orange Tree. It's a kind of old ladies' place where they serve morning coffee and afternoon tea. It's a bit twee, but Anna's Aunt Suzy runs it and she always lets us have free double hot chocolates—as long as we don't push our luck and go in there too often.

We sat at a table at the back.

"Hey girls!" Suzy greeted us. "Your usual?"

"Yes, please, Suze," Anna replied.

"It's hopeless," I said, when Suzy went off to get our drinks. "How are we going to get enough money to pay for all the new gear we need?"

"And the piercing and the tattoos, and everything else."

"Precisely! It's hopeless," I moaned.

"Hey, what's with the long faces?" Suzy said, as she returned with our cups. "Things can't be that bad."

"I don't suppose you've got any jobs here, have you?" I asked hopefully.

"Sorry, girls, no," Suzy said. "Are you looking for something, then?"

"We need to earn some cash," Anna said.

"Why's that?" Suzy arched an eyebrow. "What are you saving for?"

"Er—nothing special," I spluttered, not wanting her—or anyone for that matter—to be in on our plan.

I could see from the look on Suzy's face that she didn't believe me. She probably thought we needed it for something sinister. Fortunately, Anna jumped in to rescue me.

"We just want to be able to have money for our own stuff—you know, cinema tickets, makeup, that kind of thing."

"Oh, I see," Suzy said, looking relieved. "Well—if I hear of anyone on the High Street needing Saturday girls, I'll let you know."

When we'd finished our hot chocolates, we set off for home, walking the other way down the High Street. Both of us stopped dead when we saw the photo in the window of the Cutting Room. The Cutting Room is this super-stylish hairdresser's. It's so super stylish it's scary. I'd never been in there and I was fairly certain that Anna hadn't either. Haircuts for me tend to be my mum snipping away with her sewing scissors, not getting it even and then cutting too much off in an attempt to level it out. Nice.

"That is fantastic!" Anna said.

She was right. The photo in the window of the shop showed this girl with amazing hair. Loads of it. She looked stunning. Okay, so admittedly the girl was pretty amazing herself, but the hair just made everything look fantastic.

At the bottom of the photo was a load of blurb that explained that this stunning hair wasn't actually for real. I mean, it *looked* for real but was actually hair extensions.

"Come on." Anna grabbed my arm. "We're going in."

"No!" I panicked. "We can't! I mean—no!"

"What do you *mean* 'no'?" Anna demanded.

I opened my mouth and for a few seconds nothing came out. Then I said, "But why are we going in there? We haven't got any money! And it's, it's *cool*."

"Precisely," Anna said, looking smug. "Like us— remember? Come on—we're going in."

So we did.

All the staff were wearing jet-black clothes. Not a hair on their gorgeous shiny-haired heads was out of place. Not a speck of dandruff littered their collars.

"Can I help, girls?" smiled the receptionist. "Do you have an appointment?"

"No," Anna beamed, making me speechless with her confidence. I just stood there like a doughnut. "The photo in the window—the hair extensions . . . we were wondering how much they cost and what happens with them, you know?"

"They're fab, aren't they?" the smiley girl said.

"Great for when you're growing a style out." She leaned beautifully across her beautiful desk and picked up a brochure. "Why don't you take this; it tells you all about them. Trudie does the extensions on Thursdays and Fridays."

Smiley Girl pointed to an incredibly tall girl at the far end of the salon. Her hair reached down below her waist. It was thick and fabulous.

"Thanks!" Anna said. "We'll see you soon!"

I was still speechless. In awe of all these beautiful people and of Anna's front. Anna started to walk from the salon, until she realized that I wasn't following. She gave me a kind of sad look, then grabbed my arm and pulled me out of there. I was never going to master this.

"*How* much?" I exclaimed, as Anna read the brochure to me a few minutes later. We were sitting on the bench outside the church. *"No way!"*

"It is rather a lot, isn't it?" Even Anna looked startled at the price. "Well, they do say it takes at least four hours to do a full head of hair."

"Even so, Anna!" I retorted, despairingly.

We were silent for a moment or so and then I said, "Oh well—no hair extensions for us, then."

Anna didn't reply. She folded the leaflet up carefully and put it into her bag.

"I don't see why we should completely rule them out," she said mysteriously.

26

"Oh, come off it! Even if we *did* manage to find a couple of Saturday jobs, it would take all our wages for weeks—maybe even months—to pay for hair extensions!"

"Not if we do them ourselves," Anna decided.

"*Ourselves?* Are you kidding?"

"Well, it can't be *that* hard, can it?" Anna had a determined look on her face. "The leaflet says that acrylic hair is heat bonded to your own hair."

"And how precisely are we meant to do that?" I really wanted to know what she had in mind.

"We've got hairdryers, haven't we?"

"And the acrylic hair?"

"Easy peasy—I bet they sell it in Gammons," Anna said smugly. Gammons was the old-fashioned department store in town. "Come on—let's go and see!"

And that was how I found myself in Gammons with Anna. She found some false hair all right. Whole heads of it. What you'd call wigs. But no *strands* of acrylic hair. Then I had a brainwave. Claire's Accessories! They mainly had colored strands, but still . . . it might be worth a try.

"Okay," I said, holding some strands up to my head half an hour later. "How exactly do you propose fixing these on?"

It was obvious to even the optimistic Anna that a hairdryer was not going to be all it took. She scanned the shelves, looking almost defeated before suddenly pouncing on something.

"Got it!" she declared victoriously.

"What?" I asked, suspicious now.

"Eyelash glue!"

She wasn't joking.

Chapter Five

"So you're on for tonight, then?" Anna smiled.

"Well," I said sarcastically, "I really should stay in to scrub my feet some more . . ."

Anna laughed and, eventually, I did too. You see, we'd got the shoe dye we'd wanted and had spent Tuesday after school tarting-down my stilettos. We did it over some old newspaper because I was terrified that we'd get the dye on my bedroom carpet. Actually, we both had to admit that the shoes looked really quite cool when we'd finished with them—and they dried really quickly. So when I did my homework later on, I decided to wear them as my SJP practice for the night. Only—disaster! I got the itching problem again because of the bleach. Which made my feet sweat—

nice! And then the dye came off round the inside edges of the shoes. Now I had these really attractive black ingrained stains on my feet. Except, of course, for the bits that were red and itchy. Very attractive. Lovely, in fact.

"Whatever—so, you're still on then?" Anna said, when she'd finished laughing.

It was Wednesday afternoon and the middle of another boring week. I was going round to Anna's house after school because this was the night that we'd decided I was going to have Anna's version of hair extensions.

We'd talked for hours about which one of us should be the first to have the extensions and in the end we'd decided that, as Anna was more confident about doing them, it should be me. Don't get me wrong, I was confident about *having* them. Big hair was what I wanted. And, once Anna had perfected the extensions and done mine, then I was going to have a go on her hair another night.

"Course," I said. "Soon as I've dumped my stuff at home and changed, I'll be round. I'm going to leave a note for Mum telling her we're doing coursework."

So, an hour or so later, there I was in Anna's bedroom, sitting on a chair that we had relocated from downstairs. If I say so myself, it all looked very professional.

I was sitting in front of the mirror with a towel around my shoulders and we'd angled all the lamps in Anna's bedroom on to the chair. Just like at the hairdresser's. My hair was dry because we'd figured the glue and the hairdryer would work better if Anna was working with dry hair.

"Okay." Anna took a fat strand of brown artificial hair.

I had to admit, the color was pretty much like mine. I was beginning to feel quite excited about the thought of having a full head of Big Hair in an hour or so's time.

"I'm going to start at the back here and work my way round to the front," said Anna.

"Sounds good." I smiled.

Anna looked so together in her reflection in the mirror that I didn't doubt her skills for a minute. After all, she's brilliant at art. And hair extensions are surely just another creative art.

Anna hardly spoke as she worked away behind my head. I couldn't see the results at all from what I could view in the mirror. But she was concentrating very hard. And every time she pinched a piece of my hair together with the false hair and some glue, she kind of ruffled some of my own hair over the top of it.

It was SO boring, though. And sometimes it hurt—especially when Anna pulled at my hair like she was plucking it. The hot blasts with the hairdryer weren't much fun either and I accused Anna of burning my scalp more than once.

"What does it look like?" I asked endlessly.

All Anna would say was, "Wait until I've done the whole head. That's what it needs—the whole head, so that it's balanced out a bit."

It made me feel slightly nervous when she said that. At one point, Anna went downstairs to make a cup of coffee for us. I tried to see my reflection in the mirror but no matter what angle I tried, I just couldn't get a proper look. Although what I did see didn't look particularly natural to me. In fact, it looked a bit bushy—from about a centimeter or so from the roots. Sticking out at right angles. I said that to Anna when she came back with our coffee.

"Look, I haven't finished yet!" she accused, making me feel really bad. "Give me a chance, will you?"

"Okay—sorry." I sipped quietly from my mug.

After that I kept a close eye on everything Anna did. At one point she squirted so much of the eyelash glue that a drop of it—a large drop—plopped onto the floor. We had to wipe it up really quickly.

"My mum'll kill me if that leaves a stain," Anna said, panicking.

Other than that, having hair extensions done is just boring. I got stiff and my bum started to ache from sitting on the chair for so long. It was okay for Anna because she was bobbing around and clearly enjoying herself.

After an age, Anna started to get closer to the bits around the side of my head that I could see.

"I can see the joins," I said to Anna, my voice raised in panic.

"What do you mean?" Anna asked, as if she didn't know what I meant and didn't really expect me to answer. But I did.

"The joins—where the false hair is joined to my hair. You can see it! There are joins!" I was standing up now, trying to angle round to get a better view of the back.

"Well, there have to be joins, don't there?" Anna said, pursing her lips like she does when she's being told off at school. "I mean, I can't attach your hair to the extensions without there being some kind of join."

"But I thought the whole point of hair extensions was that you couldn't see the difference between the real hair and the extensions." I was really worried now.

"I haven't finished," Anna snapped. "When I have— if you'll just sit back down and let me, that is—I can fold your own hair over the extensions. Now, will you sit down?"

I did, but I didn't feel happy about it.

We had both had a sense of humor failure. Anna worked in silence. Eventually she said, "Right, it's done."

She'd stopped the hair extensions somewhere around

by my ears and she ruffled the hair at the front so that it was swept back a bit.

I stood up to take a closer look in the mirror. As I did, a lump of hair extension fell to the floor.

"Oh," Anna said, grabbing it quickly and hiding it behind her back. "So, what do you think?"

"Have you got another mirror—you know, so that I can see it from the back? Like in the hairdresser's?"

"Umm . . . only this one," Anna said, holding up a little mirror.

I couldn't see much but what I *could* see looked just as bad as the clumpy bits I'd seen at the sides.

"No way!" I said. "No way, Anna!"

"What do you mean? You've got long hair, haven't you?"

"Not the kind of long hair I wanted!" I said, feeling freaked out by my new appearance.

Anna looked at me, not nearly as pleased with herself as she had been at the start.

"Well, it is a *bit* patchy, I suppose. We could always get some more false hair tomorrow and finish it off then," she suggested.

"You must be mad if you think I'm going to go to school tomorrow looking like this!" I couldn't believe that Anna was serious. "You've got to get this lot off."

"That's not fair!" Anna said. "It's taken me ages!"

"And it's not fair to leave me looking like this!"

Anna didn't say anything for a while. Then she said, "Okay, you're right. It looks pants. Total pants and I'm really sorry. We've got to get it off. Come on—let me start."

I sat back down in front of the mirror and Anna tugged at some of the false hair at the back.

"Oww! That hurts!"

"Sorry—I'm just trying to get it off," Anna said, trying again.

"Ouch! It *majorly* hurts!"

The hair wouldn't budge.

"Well—I suppose you got that bit right, at least. It's certainly attached," I said sarcastically.

Anna tried to take off other bits of hair but none seemed to move.

"I think we need to wash it," she suggested.

"Okay," I said. I just wanted it to look like my hair again.

"Look—I'll check Joey's not hanging around outside and then you can go into the shower and wash it all off."

I groaned. That was all I needed—Joey seeing me like this.

So I had the shower. I shampooed my hair. The only problem was that though the water made the false hair go completely fuzzy and wrinkled, not much of it actually came off. And, when I tried to dry it with the hairdryer there was a terrible smell of burning and smoke started to come out of it.

"This is getting even worse!" I wailed.

I noticed that Anna didn't disagree with me. She was about to say something when there was a knock on the door and her mum came in.

"Oh my God!" She put her hand up to her mouth. "What on earth have you two been doing?"

Chapter Six

Fifteen minutes later we were down in the living room. After explanations, looks of disbelief, and me and Anna feeling like complete and utter planks, Anna's mum rang mine.

"No—I insist," she was saying. "I feel totally responsible for this happening in my house. After all, Anna was the one who did it. I'll call that new hairdresser's in town and see if I can get an appointment for Beth first thing in the morning." She listened to my mum for a while, then said, "I really don't think that Beth can go to school looking like she does."

When she got off the phone, Anna's mum said that mine was going to collect me on her way home from work. Which was a relief because I really couldn't face going out in public looking like this. Anna's mum was so angry with her that she could barely speak. I think the only reason she was speaking to me was because I looked so awful. She obviously felt sorry for me. When Joey came in, I saw his jaw drop. It was a nightmare! Thankfully, he didn't laugh. I don't know why, because I would have if I'd been him. I'd wanted hair to die for and now I'd got hair that made me want to die. Talk about a bad hair day . . .

It got worse. Anna's mum was insistent that I go to the Cutting Room to get my hair sorted out first thing in the morning. Problem was, when she rang them, they were fully booked all morning. The best they could do was straight after school. I thought my mum might let me stay at home for the day. As if! She said that there was nothing wrong with me that a headscarf wouldn't cover up. Sometimes life is so not fair.

Worse still, when I got home that evening my disgusting baby brother spent the entire time taking the mickey out of me. And when my dad got home, he laughed so much I thought he'd wet himself. Just brilliant all round, really. Whose idea was it to try and look like Beyoncé, anyway?

After a day of Total World Humiliation during which practically every teacher and every kid at school asked me what was wrong with my hair, Anna and I finally made our way to the Cutting Room.

"I don't know why you're looking so miserable," Anna said as we hopped off the bus in the High Street. "After all, you're going to the trendiest hairdresser's for miles around."

"Only because of the disaster attached to my head!" I wailed. "Sure—I'd love to be going to the Cutting Room if I was going in looking more like a human being in the first place. Instead I'm going in looking like a bad version of Marge Simpson."

"Oh lighten up, Beth!" Anna replied. "I've said I'm sorry—and I truly am. Just try to think about how fab you'll look when you come out."

"I suppose so," I grunted, not totally convinced.

We were getting close to the hairdresser's. I felt stupid. Here I was, about to go into a place that should have made me feel good, and all I wanted was for the earth to swallow me up.

We didn't need to introduce ourselves to the receptionist. She just took one look at us as we walked in and said, "Ah. You're here."

I felt the gaze of everyone in the salon on me as I was ushered through to a seat.

"Everyone knows!" I hissed at Anna as the receptionist left, promising that Nicky would be with us in a minute.

"Don't be daft!" Anna hissed back. "Why would anyone in here be interested in you?"

"Oh, thanks!"

Anna's cheeks went slightly pink. "I didn't mean it like that! Hey—look at that guy over there. Is he fit, or what?"

There was a cute boy pulling towels out of a cupboard on the far side of the salon.

"Not bad," I agreed. "Which one do you think Nicky is?"

Anna didn't reply because she was too busy trying out her Enigmatic Smile technique on Cute Boy. She got cringe-makingly worse at it as he started to walk across the salon, coming dangerously close to Anna's Boy-net Zone. Just as she looked like she was going to pounce, Cute Boy stopped next to my chair.

"Hi there! I'm Nicky—I gather you're Beth."

Result!

Nicky was to die for. I'd wanted hair to die for and now I'd ended up with a hairdresser to die for! Not a bad exchange, I suppose. I explained to Nicky what had happened. Or at least I tried to explain to Nicky what had happened, only Anna was, quite literally, falling over herself in her rush to tell him the story of my hair and the extensions.

"You poor thing!" Nicky sympathized, giving me a cute grin.

40

"Can you get rid of this lot?" I asked. "But I really, really don't want to have my hair too short."

"Don't panic," Nicky said, running his fingers through my hair. At least he tried to, but the gloop of the glue and the acrylic fuzz stopped him. "I think we should be able to sort most of it out for you. Come on—let's start by washing it."

He gave me a wink and I followed him over to the basin.

No way was Anna going to leave us alone. She followed Nicky around the salon like a puppy chasing a loo roll. Boy, was she in flirt mode. *Major* flirt mode.

"Hey Nicky, that shampoo smells lovely—what is it?"

"Hey, Nicky, what are you doing now?"

"How long have you worked here, Nicky?"

"Did you always want to be a hairdresser, Nicky? I've always loved playing with people's hair—wouldn't mind being a hairdresser myself."

What was she *like*? I'd never heard of this ambition to be a hairdresser—she'd never shown the slightest interest, at least not before her moment of Hair Extension Madness. Honestly, she was shameless! I could hardly get a word in edgeways.

About an hour later, I was still sitting in front of the mirror, a carpet of the acrylic gunk around my feet. My hair was looking less fuzzy, but Nicky had

had to take the scissors to one or two long strands that still had chunks of acrylic stuck to them. If he hadn't been so cute, I think I might have cried. After all, one of the things on our list was to *grow* our hair—and now I had even less than when I'd started.

It was almost as if Nicky could read my mind because he said, "Don't worry about it, Beth—I'll show you how to style your hair so you can make the most of it."

I smiled at him in relief and gratitude. Sure enough, it wasn't long before Nicky was starting to level off the length of my hair and using a razor to make feathery shapes where he'd had to cut the longer pieces.

"It'll help the hair to blend," he explained.

And all the while Anna was chipping in with her comments and cooing about how clever Nicky was.

Nicky plugged in the hairdryer and started to dry my new cut. I began to see some shape in it. And I liked it. Nicky was making my hair look good! I got up the courage to interrupt Anna's chatter and ask Nicky for some tips on treatments to help our hair look good. He mentioned a couple for strength and shine.

"Anyway," Nicky said, "even after all this glue stuff, your hair is in really good condition, Beth."

Result!

By the time Nicky had finished with my hair, it looked really good—dead straight and shimmery in the light. Nicky held up a mirror so that I could see the back of my hair reflected in the mirror in front of me.

"Okay?" he asked with a cheeky grin. "I'll give you some treatments to take home with you—to keep it looking gorgeous."

Nicky had said that my hair looked gorgeous! I accepted the goodie bag of hair stuff with gushing thanks and put on my coat, spluttering my good-byes.

"See you again, Beth!" Nicky said.

"Yes," I said wistfully, knowing that I would never be able to afford a haircut in the Cutting Room again.

"And, Anna," Nicky said, "we've got a vacancy for a Saturday girl, if you're interested."

"Interested?" Anna practically glowed. "When do you want me to start?"

"Well—we've got a big wedding party to do next Saturday. That's not the best day to start. How about the Saturday after that?" Nicky smiled.

I couldn't believe it! Even after causing all this trouble, Anna was coming up smelling of roses! How did my best friend do it?

Chapter Seven

"I've got a job!" Anna squealed, as we left the Cutting Room. "Isn't that great?"

"Fantastic," I agreed sarcastically. "Now you can afford to buy all the things on our list and I can't."

"Don't be daft," Anna said, giving me a hug as we walked home. "Listen, you've got the kind of hairstyle we normally only see in magazines, while my hair is a total mess. In fact, I reckon I did you a favor by mucking up your hair in the first place!"

"Only you, Anna! Only you could say something like that!" But I couldn't help laughing.

"What?" Anna said, raising an eyebrow at me.

"You got great hair, didn't you? And you didn't even have to pay for it!"

I smiled and linked arms with her. She was right, after all!

My hair was still looking pretty amazing the next morning. It was luscious, shiny, and had this swingy sort of cut that made it sway when I walked. Especially when I bounced my head as I walked. Which I did. A lot. As I walked to meet Anna at the bus stop.

"Nice hairdo!" Anna said, as if she'd never seen it before.

"Thank you!" I beamed.

There's something about having really cool hair. It makes you feel loads better about yourself. I felt like I was somehow invincible, even though I was only on my way to school for registration, then a session of double Science.

At school, Frankie was still jabbering on about her new modeling career. There had obviously been a big, new development.

"So, they've told me that there'll be work for me whenever I want it," Frankie was telling the class as Anna and I walked in. "Of course my dad is being ultra boring and saying that I can only work in the holidays. But Mum talked to me when he wasn't around and said that if someone like Armani or Testino wants to work with me then it goes without saying that, of course, she'll let me go whenever or wherever it is and Dad will just have to put up and shut up."

"Oh, Frankie, that's so fantastic," crooned Trish, one of the Frankie-ettes.

"Armani? Testino?" Anna whispered to me. "What *is* she talking about?"

I shrugged and listened for more explanation. Fortunately, Izzie, one of the more normal girls in the class—not one of the Frankie set—asked the one question I was dying to know the answer to.

"So what happened, Frankie? How come you're going to work with Mario Testino?"

"Don't you know?" said Vic, looking smug. Whatever it was, Frankie's little gang of fans was basking in her shared glory.

"I wouldn't be asking if I did, would I?" Izzie smiled, just managing to hold back the sarcasm.

"Frankie's been to see the model agent!" Sylvie said excitedly.

"At one of the top agencies in London!" Trish finished.

I groaned out loud and Anna jabbed me in the ribs.

For the final ten minutes before Registration, Trish, Vic, Sylvie, and Frankie told us all about how Frankie had been up in town with her mum yesterday evening to have some photos taken and now, ker-CHING! Frankie had been signed up as a model. She was, apparently, simply waiting for her first booking.

I looked at Anna. She looked at me. Luckily there was no time to say anything—except "Yes, miss," because, thankfully, at that very moment, Miss Anstey arrived to take registration.

Frankie and the Frankie-ettes spent every available moment that day discussing the hot topic of Frankie being a potential supermodel. Even the teachers seemed to know about it by lunchtime.

Anna and I wandered through the canteen, trying to find a place that was as far away from them as possible. It was hard to avoid the gossip, though. Even people who didn't know Frankie were chatting amongst themselves about how someone in our school was about to become world famous and mega rich.

"Hey, look!" Anna said, grinning. "How convenient that the only spare seats just happen to be near Baz and Greg. On the very same table, no less!"

Baz and Greg were in Year Twelve and they were gorgeous. Although it would be fair to admit that Baz was the MORE gorgeous of the two.

In nine months, we'd done nothing about our mission to go out with Baz and Greg. But hey! Here we were now—me with my fab new hairdo, Anna with her groovy new job—perhaps it was time to put our plan into action!

"Mind if we sit here?" Anna said, not leaving room for any answer other than "no."

We took possession of those two chairs as if our lives depended on it. I gave my hair a pat and Anna flicked a blonde curl behind her ear, then placed her elbows on the table, cupping her chin with her hands. She opened her brown eyes as wide as they would go and leaned toward Baz.

"I see you chose the same meal as me," she said to him, ignoring Greg.

So that was how it was. As far as Anna was concerned, Greg was my "date" this lunchtime. Still, I didn't mind too much.

"Uh, yeah," Baz said, slightly puzzled by Anna's interest in the gray slop on his plate.

"So, do you come here often?" Anna said, laughing rather too hysterically at her pathetic joke.

"Only if we can't avoid it," Greg replied sarcastically.

I couldn't think of anything to say. I felt like a rabbit caught in headlights. My brain struggled to come up with something.

"Can you pass the salt please, Greg?" I managed at last, with an accompanying bounce of my hair.

"See you've dropped the headscarf look," Greg said, nodding toward my head.

48

"Oh, this? Yes." He'd noticed my hair! Maybe this list thing was working. . . . Then Baz had to ruin it.

"So what's all this about your mate Frankie getting a modeling contract, then?"

On the bus home that afternoon, Anna said, "Even Baz and Greg were talking about Frankie! I can't bear it."

"But Greg noticed my hair!" I said, smugly.

"What?"

"Greg spotted my hair! He said I'd dropped the headscarf look."

"Not *quite* the same as spotting your hair," Anna said, I thought a little too unkindly.

"Well . . . I know he didn't exactly say my hair looked *nice*. But he did at least notice it."

"You mean he noticed that you didn't look like someone with a paper bag over their head," Anna concluded.

I decided to let it go. "That Frankie really gets up my nose!" I wailed, as we hopped off the bus at the High Street.

"You and me both!" Anna agreed.

We walked along in silence for a moment. Then I spotted the sign.

"Look!" I exclaimed. "The new supermarket!

The one by the traffic lights—it's just about to open. They're advertising for Saturday staff! I'm going in!"

Anna grinned. "Go for it, Beth!"

So I did. And I came out with a job. I was starting in two weeks' time—the first Saturday that the shop would be open!

Chapter Eight

By Friday morning, I couldn't leave my hair any longer without washing it. As I'd suspected, my attempts at blow drying were not as good as the Cutting Room's. Anna offered to blow dry it for me, but after her last attempt at hairdressing I said no. Like SO no.

"Okay," Anna said, as we hopped off the bus to walk to school. "Our final free Saturday tomorrow. What are we going to do with it?"

Next weekend, Anna and I were both due to start our jobs. And it had dawned on me in the last couple of days that I was now going to have only one morning a week to lie in. Still, the money that I was going to earn would easily make up for it. Plus Anna and I were hoping that our lunch hours would coincide so that we could spend them together. That, at least, would be worth getting up for.

"I don't know," I replied. "Maybe we should just have a lazy day?"

"No way!" Anna exclaimed. "Our last Saturday is not going to be wasted!"

Natch. It had been a stupid thing to say. You see, Anna hates sitting around doing nothing. She's easily bored – and, when Anna's bored, she usually starts plotting something.

"Shall we go shopping then? I mean, window-shopping? You know, to spot all the things we're going to buy once we've got the money from working?"

"Maybe . . ." Anna was pensive. I could tell she was coming up with one of her Good Ideas. "In fact, YES. We *will* go shopping. Only not around here. Let's go to Oxford Street."

We lived in a little town at the very end of one of the Underground lines into London. Oxford Street seemed a long way off.

"Oxford Street?" I said. "Why Oxford Street? Especially if we haven't got any money . . ."

"Because, Beth," Anna said, hooking her arm through mine, "that's where the big Top Shop is! Which is where a certain irritating schoolgirl was recently spotted by a model scout . . ."

⊚

"Okay," Anna said the next morning, as we waited for a tube train. "I've been practicing the Walk."

"What walk?" I asked, bemused.

"The Modeling Walk, silly," Anna replied, as our tube drew into the platform. "According to the magazine I read, what we have to do is put one foot down almost on top of the other before lifting that one from the floor. That way it gives us a sort of swagger."

"Oh, right," I said, not sure that I understood exactly what Anna meant.

"I'll show you when we get off."

When at last we got to our stop, we stepped onto the platform and busied ourselves people-watching. There was one girl with the longest legs I've ever seen —I'm tall, but we're talking giraffe here—and she looked irritatingly gorgeous in a pair of skin-tight jeans, as she hung around for her train. Another girl with a long skirt and a chunky belt slinked past us, looking cool. I suddenly wished I wasn't wearing a boring black top and my oldest pair of scruffy jeans. I made a mental note about the way their outfits were assembled and promised myself that I'd try and adapt some of my clothes along the same lines when I got home.

Anna and I headed toward the escalator. As we did,

Anna tried out the Modeling Walk. It was a bit over the top—and a bloke coming down the escalator saw us and started to giggle.

"It might be too much for the Underground," Anna said sniffily, as we reached the top, "but I can assure you it's made Kate Moss rich! Come on, we've got to go this way."

I zipped up my jacket and trailed out of the exit after Anna. "Look," I said, pointing to a sign. "It's over there."

I took a deep breath and sucked in my cheeks. At the same time, I opened my blue-gray eyes as wide as I could.

Anna looked at me.

"Very good, Beth!" she said. "You've been practicing too!"

It was true. I'd been rereading all my magazine back copies to pick up tips on how to get the supermodel look. If Frankie could do it, then so could Anna and I!

I caught my reflection in a shop window. Okay, so I looked a bit startled. But my eyes were BIG. Ker-CHING!

Once we were inside the shop, I wondered what exactly we were meant to do in order to be spotted by these model people.

"Look at clothes," Anna suggested helpfully. "Just look like the average shopper—but remember that these two average shoppers happen to be supermodels-in-waiting!"

So we did. We looked at jeans, tops, and jewelery. We looked at makeup and dresses and skirts. But no one tapped us on the shoulder and said how stunning we were. No one rushed over and took a photo of us, either. And, after a couple of hours, our "window shopping" got more than a little boring, to say the least.

"This is no good, is it?" Anna confessed, as we sloped off to the café for a rest.

"No," I agreed. "And I am also completely starving!"

"Me too," Anna said. "Have you got any money?"

"No—after the tube fare and this coffee I'll be skint."

"Oh well—think of the weight we must be losing."

"Like you need to lose weight," I said sarcastically. Anna was skinny, verging on gangly, even though she had an appetite like a horse. It was very annoying.

We sat in silence for a while and sipped at our coffee. Most of the other people in the café were just like us. Other girls about our age, some pretty, some spotty, some with greasy hair. Most of them with their mums and a heap of carrier bags. Maybe that was the way to do it—bring your mum. At least then you might get some clothes out of it, if nothing else.

"Come on," Anna said, when we'd got nothing but dregs left in our cups. "Let's go back to the jeans section and do some more cheek-sucking."

We trooped off. The good thing about the cheek-sucking is that it has the side-effect of drawing in your stomach. Neither of us really had a fat stomach, but I did have an empty one: It was rumbling loudly and embarrassingly as we took another look at the jeans.

"Sorry," I said, blushing.

"Beth!" Anna hissed, as a girl moved away from us, frowning.

"I can't help it!" I explained. "Look, can't we just go home? Then we could at least raid the biscuit tin."

"Let's give it a little longer," Anna said. "Please?"

I sighed and pretended that I was interested in another pair of denims. That was when I saw him. A man. Staring. He was looking at us intently.

"Anna!" I whispered. "Look!" I gave a nod of my head in the man's direction.

Anna looked up. "Do the cheek thing! Quickly!"

So we did—plus I gazed my widest eyes at him. Which was hard because, what with the breathing in and the hunger pangs, I was beginning to feel pretty faint.

Anna, meanwhile, had gone slightly mad. She was doing her Modeling Walk as, still gazing at the man, she slunk across to another rack of jeans. She looked a complete prat, if you ask me. I saw the man kind of tilt his head to one side, and mutter into his hand.

A minute later, I felt a tap on my shoulder. Before

I could turn round, a woman's voice said, "Can you come this way, please?"

"What?" I spluttered, my heart pounding. "Anna?" I looked around for her.

She was being whisked off by another woman to the other side of the shop. Could this be it? Had we been "spotted"?

We had, but not quite in the way we'd intended.

"Well, girls," the bossier of the women said, as we were escorted out of the shop doors half an hour later. "Enjoy the rest of your afternoon."

"Oh, we will!" Anna said, in her cockiest voice. "NOT!"

"Let's just go, shall we?" I muttered, grabbing Anna and walking her back toward the Underground.

"That was one of the most humiliating moments of my life!" Anna declared. "Imagine them thinking we were shoplifters!"

"What a disaster," I agreed. So much for being "spotted."

"How come Frankie was picked up by a modeling agency and all we get are store detectives?" Anna demanded. "What makes her so lucky?"

"I don't know." I sighed. I couldn't think straight. It was true—Frankie did seem to have all the luck. "But I don't suppose Frankie would tell us about the bad stuff, would she?"

"I s'pose not," Anna huffed. "Oh NO!"

"What now?" I asked.

"My worst nightmare has now truly happened!"

"What?" I wanted to know.

"Over there!" Anna pointed back at the shop entrance. "It's them!"

"Who?" I asked. I couldn't keep up.

"Baz and Greg!" Anna explained. "They're standing there, smiling—correction *laughing*—at us. Beth—they must have seen it all!"

Embarrassed? I could have died. . . .

Chapter Nine

Baz and Greg were full of it. How had we managed to be so stupid that we'd looked like shoplifters? And why were we in Oxford Street anyway, if we didn't have any money? Could we possibly have been in the shop because of what had happened to Frankie?

They followed us down into the Underground and went on and on. They even hopped onto the same tube as us and carried on as it went into the tunnel. *Ha ha*, they sniggered. Anna and I sat in silence as the train rumbled along—we didn't even talk to each other, though Anna did raise her eyebrows at me as the two boys sat and laughed at us from the other side of the carriage. The more they mocked, the more irritated we got. Would they tell everyone at school? That really *would* be bad.

When we got to our stop to change onto a bus for the rest of the journey home, Greg and Baz followed us like puppies. Only, unlike puppies, these two boys had suddenly lost their charm.

"Planning to pay your bus fares, you two?" Greg asked smugly. "Or are you going to fare dodge as well as shoplift?"

The pair of them were like little kids, laughing at their own jokes. I saw red.

"For a start we were NOT shoplifting," I spat. "It was a mistake—okay?"

"Oo-er," said Baz, smirking.

"And anyway," I continued, "what were you two doing in the girls' section? Hey?"

They stopped laughing then. I must have hit a nerve.

"Way to go, Beth!" said Anna, realizing I was on to something.

"Come on," I said, demanding an answer. "What *were* you doing in the shop? You must have been there if you saw us get picked up, but I can't see any shopping bags on you two, either."

"Oh, I get it!" Anna smiled suddenly, as the penny began to drop with her as well as me. "You were there to see if you could be picked up by a modeling agency too, weren't you?"

"No . . . ," Baz spluttered, a flush rising up his neck.

"We were just seeing what kind of things were there," Greg said, desperately thinking on his feet.

"Yes," said Baz, picking up the thread. "It's my sister's birthday soon. I was looking for ideas."

"And maybe hoping that you might just be spotted as a male model at the same time?" I said.

Baz and Greg denied it, but they weren't laughing anymore.

"Gotcha!" Anna said, satisfied at last. "Come on, Beth. Let's go home!"

And we jumped on a bus and left them behind.

At Anna's, we decided to get back on track with our list and spent the rest of the afternoon giving each other beauty treatments. I had this idea for trying out nail decorations and Anna agreed that if I did her fingernails, she'd do my toes. And while we were doing those, we decided to have a face pack each.

"I found this in the bathroom," Anna said, brandishing a tube of something called Face Facts.

"What is it?"

"Oh, I dunno—some kind of face mask," Anna replied. "According to the label it 'puts back the nature that nature has taken out.' That sound okay?"

"Sounds fine to me," I said. "But isn't your mum going to notice that we've nicked it?"

"Nah," Anna said, waving the tube around in

61

disagreement. "There's loads here and we won't be using that much, will we?"

"So, what do we have to do?" I took the tube and read the label. Apparently, we slapped the cream stuff on and left it to dry before peeling it off to reveal a fresh new face. "Spooky!" I said. "Shall I go first?"

"Okay—but don't forget to take your makeup off!" Anna warned.

"Like I don't realize that?" I said, full of mock-offence, as I grabbed Anna's cleansing wipes from her dressing table.

Once the pack was applie—it was a rather sickly lurid green—we got carried away with the nails. Our original idea of doing each other at the same time was a non-starter because, of course, we both discovered that we couldn't. Not least because I couldn't do Anna's nails while they were meant to be doing mine—if you see what I mean. So, in the end, we compromised and did one part of each other's treatment at a time. I started on Anna's nails first, doing her cuticles, and following a kind of "recipe" for a manicure that Anna had found in a magazine.

"Oww!" Anna wailed as I dug under her nails. "That hurts!"

"Well, I can't leave dirt under them, can I?" I exclaimed.

"Okay!" Anna protested. "But I think you'll find it's not dirt but paint from yesterday's art lesson."

"Whatever," I said. "I can't leave it there or it will ruin the nail art. And aren't we meant to take the face mask off soon?"

"Oh—I don't think the timing's that important," Anna said. "Anyway—it's a little difficult to take off the mask when I've got wet nails, no?"

"I take your point," I agreed. "We can do the masks later."

I really enjoyed doing Anna's nails. I'd put these tiny sequins onto each nail, with a dark blue base coat which made the sequins look like little stars. It was painstaking stuff, but Anna was more than happy to sit back while I worked. When the sequins were all in place and seemed to be dry, I painted a coat of transparent top coat over them to protect them and give a final shine.

"You'll have to sit there until they're completely dry," I warned. "Or they'll smudge."

"Suits me," Anna said. "Fancy making me a coffee though?"

"Ha ha, very funny," I said. "You don't think I'm going to venture downstairs with this mask on my face, do you?"

"Good point." Anna giggled.

So we sat and waited, listening to a CD and reading magazines for a while. I could have taken my mask off, but wanted to wait a few minutes so we could do both together.

63

But then there was a knock at Anna's door. Why did Anna's mum always come in when we were up to something?

"Who is it?" Anna asked.

"Me!" came Joey's reply. "Just wondered if you fancied a cup of coffee?"

And, before Anna could reply, Joey was in the room.

"Oh!" all three of us said at once.

"What are you two up to *now*?" Joey asked, staring at our faces.

"Just doing our nails," I said limply, as if the gunk on our faces was invisible to him.

"Of course," Joey said, smiling slightly but not mentioning the face masks. "So—want some coffee?"

"Yes, please—two, please," Anna commanded. "See you in a mo."

"Sure."

And Joey went, closing the door behind him.

"That was a close one," I said, breathing out. "We must look pretty ridiculous—but Joey didn't say anything!"

"Oh, it's only Joey," Anna said, dismissively.

"But we've got green cack on our faces!" I protested. "If my brother saw us looking like this he'd milk it for all it's worth!"

"Like I said," Anna sighed. "It's only Joey—don't worry about it."

"Well," I said. "I'm taking mine off now."

I pulled at the green, which had dried into a transparent sort of plastic. Fortunately, it came off easily. Anna did hers too—and finished just in time before Joey came back in the room. This time, he knocked and waited for us to say he could come in.

"Wow!" Joey said, as he handed us our mugs and caught sight of our nails. "They look cool."

"Thanks," I said.

"Good, aren't they?" Anna said, waggling her fingers so they caught the light and sparkled all the more. "Beth—you could get yourself a job doing this, if I say so myself."

"Thanks." I blushed.

"Praise indeed," Joey said. "Anna doesn't say things like that to just anyone."

"Oh yawn, yawn," Anna said, sarcastically. "Can we help you with anything else, Joey?"

"No," he said. "Looks like I'd better be off. Only, let me just . . ."

Joey leaned toward me and put his hand in my hair. I felt myself blushing and didn't know what to say. What was he doing?

"Joey!" Anna squealed. "What are you up to?"

"Just getting the rest of this mask off," Joey said, pulling some of the elastic green plastic from behind my ear.

Now I really *was* blushing. "Thanks," I said quietly.

Then Joey was gone. No sarcasm. No laughing. Just gone. My brother would never have behaved like that in a million years. Anna didn't know how lucky she was.

Chapter Ten

Even if I say so myself, the nails experience was pretty good. I'm not at all bad at manicures and I enjoyed doing Anna's nails. She wasn't bad either—she'd painted a little daisy on each of my big toenails. Unfortunately for Anna, though, she'd got it in the neck from her mum when she'd gone into the bathroom to do a face pack and couldn't find it. When she'd discovered it half used-up in Anna's bedroom she'd apparently gone ape. Not that Anna seemed too bothered. Even I couldn't believe how chilled she was sometimes.

We spent Sunday in my bedroom, using the hair treatments that Nicky had given me. We both emerged with glossy, healthy-looking hair and for once we managed not to make fools of ourselves in front of other people. We spent some time going over the list too. We seemed to have got the nails sussed. We'd even got the jobs—although the loads of dosh bit had some way to go. The hair was looking more promising than it had a few weeks ago, but it still had a long way to go. Shoes—well, sort of okay. Going out with hotties—well, Baz and Greg had been a disaster. But who wanted those losers anyway?

The following week was spent in excited anticipation of starting work the next Saturday. How we were going to spend the money, where we were going to go shopping when we got our first pay packets. It was the main topic of conversation on the bus to and from school every day.

"Jeans," Anna said, decisively, on one of our journeys. "I'm going to buy the best jeans I can afford—ones that make my legs look fantastically long and slim."

"Shoes," I suggested. "Shoes I can wear under the jeans I've already got, and which will make me look taller."

"You mean you're not happy with your streaky stilettos?" Anna grinned.

In our heads, we created long lists of what we wanted to buy: makeup, clothes, earrings, more clothes, shoes (lots), more makeup—everything, really. And we were determined to look fab in all of them.

"So, what are you going to wear to work tomorrow?" Anna asked me, as we set off for home on Friday afternoon.

"Nothing special," I said. "I've got to wear an overall so it's not like I'm going to have my clothes on parade, is it?"

"I suppose not," Anna agreed. "I've got to wear a Cutting Room shirt like all the other staff. They've also asked me to wear black trousers or a skirt—I'm going to borrow something from Mum. And yes, before you say it, I have asked!"

I felt slightly jealous of Anna. Her job was way more glamorous than mine. Being in a posh hairdresser's, working with gorgeous people, helping create fantastic hair . . . somehow stacking tins of baked beans didn't quite match up.

"But think of the great exercise," Anna said.

"What exercise?" I asked.

"Stretching up to stack those tins," Anna stated authoritatively. "It'll give you arms like Jennifer Aniston. *And* help you with your hamstring stretch."

I hadn't thought about that aspect of working in the supermarket. Maybe toned arms *would* make up for the disgusting overall, but somehow I doubted it . . .

In the end, I decided to wear jeans and a T-shirt to the supermarket. And a fat waste of time it was bothering to even think about it. Because at the supermarket my supervisor told me that it was company policy not to let you wear trousers under your overalls (which were a sickly brown, like dog poo) so I had to take my jeans off. Which would have been just about okay, except that I was wearing socks, not tights. Great! So the first thing I ended up spending my hard-earned cash on was a pair of brown tights in my tea-break. How cool is that? NOT!

I hadn't anticipated how monotonous a day at the supermarket could be. A whole day, that is. First I was taught (yes, like at school) how to find my way around the stock room. All this boring stuff about health and safety and keeping out of the way of forklift trucks and things. Like *der*! Then all this stuff about how to collect things from the stock room and take them out to the shop. After that I was told how to stack the shelves (like *please*!). My reward for doing all these things well was to be taught how to work the till—ker-CHING! But first I had to earn this "treat" by proving I could stack those shelves.

One tin of baked beans is pretty much like any other when you're plonking them on shelves. Dull.

You take the tin from the trolley and put it on the shelf. And then you keep on doing that until the shelf is full and the trolley is empty. All day.

I changed out of my awful overall and rushed out to see Anna for lunch.

"So, Gorgeous," Anna said, when we met at the chip shop (we'd decided that chips were all we could afford if we were serious about saving our wages for better things). "Tell me what you've been up to."

I did.

"Pants, eh?" she commiserated. "It can't be *that* bad."

"I might have exaggerated just a teensy bit," I allowed. "Maybe small pants, rather than big pants. I mean, the people are friendly . . . a bit of a laugh, even . . . and it's a way of getting some dosh. But you should see the uniform!"

Anna giggled.

"So," I continued. "How's *your* morning been?"

"Well," Anna said slowly. "Actually I feel really mean saying this, but it's been good—great, even."

"Seriously?" I said. "I'm really pleased for you." Honestly, I meant it. "So what did you get up to?"

"I got shown how to wash hair—and I mean properly, with a bit of a head massage at the end,"

Anna said, going into "serious hairdresser" mode. "Nicky says I'm a natural."

"Oh, Nicky does, does he?" I said, grinning.

Anna blushed. "Well, you've got to admit he's dead cute," she said.

"I know he is," I agreed, looking at my watch. "Come on, finish your chips and tell me everything else you've got up to, quick. I've got some serious shelves to stack this afternoon!"

You'd be amazed how many people shop on Saturday afternoons—and how much food they buy to shovel down their families' throats. It seemed like I'd only just stacked one shelf before the next one was empty. I got to work on the breakfast cereal aisle in the afternoon. I mean, how exciting is that? People just can't buy enough of the stuff! But at least the boxes were light. I got a bit worried about myself after a while because I started to get a thing about how neat "my" shelves were looking as opposed to Mo's. Mo was the person I shared the breakfast cereal aisle with. Sad or what?

What with the cornflakes and the greedy shoppers, the afternoon went loads quicker than the morning. The best bit was being given my pay packet at the end of the afternoon tea-break. I put the cash straight in my purse and locked it up in my personal locker. Result!

⊚

But boy, did my feet ache that night! I kicked my shoes off as soon as I got home—I couldn't believe how much they hurt!

"Err! Stink!" yelled my disgusting baby brother, as I slumped down on the sofa. He grabbed a cushion and held it over his face.

"Oh, thanks!" I said, but then blushed as I got a waft of my feet.

He was right—they *did* stink. I quickly poked them back into my shoes and stood up to head for the kitchen.

"That's enough, Will," my mum said, giving me a sympathetic look. "So, how was your first day, love?"

"Okay," I replied. "Hard work. But okay really. I need a coffee, though—want one?"

"I'll come and help you," Mum said and followed me out of the room.

After I chatted with Mum for a bit, I went upstairs for a long hot soak in the bath. I read my magazine while I lay there in the steaming, bubbly water. But I was feeling a bit sleepy and the magazine slipped and ended up all soggy. Rats! So I hung the magazine over the radiator to let it dry and got out of the bath.

Back in my bedroom, I'd just put a CD on when my phone rang. It was Anna.

"I'm completely knackered!" she said.

"Me too," I replied. "What's the point of earning money if we're too tired to go out and spend it?"

Anna laughed. "Well, everyone else with a Saturday job seems to manage it. Perhaps we'll get used to it."

"Huh," I grunted.

"So, what are we going to do tonight?" Anna asked.

"Do? Are you kidding?" I spluttered. "Surely you're not suggesting we go out tonight?"

There was a moment's silence. "No—you're right. I'm just too tired to go out. I'm going to watch a film on TV."

"Me too," I agreed. "But don't you dare tell Frankie on Monday!"

Chapter Eleven

I *was literally* too whacked to do much more than watch telly that night. But I did give myself a hand treatment I'd read about in a magazine. It said that if you slathered your hands with olive oil it would make them all soft and sensual. My mum's always got loads of olive oil in the kitchen so, natch, when the Saturday night movie was over, I grabbed a bottle of it and went up to my room.

I lay back on my bed, a book on my lap, and glooped the oil out of the bottle and onto my hands. Admittedly, I did smell like I was about to be lightly fried with some garlic and onions, but I kept thinking that this was going to give me hands to die for and, just as important, this was a treat that was FREE!

75

Once I'd got the gloopy oil out of the bottle my hands were pretty greasy, even though I hadn't used that much, so it was pretty gunky putting the lid back on the bottle. Never mind, I thought, I'll wipe it up later. That turned out to be problem number one.

Problem number two was how to turn the pages of the book I was reading with hands covered in cooking oil. Soon my book was covered in oily fingerprints, the oil leaving transparent patches on the pages. Soft, sumptuous hands, I reminded myself, ignoring my irritation at now having a book that looked like it was about to be cooked too.

After a short while, I found myself nodding off. I couldn't believe it! How horrific. Nodding off was what my mum and dad did when they were sitting on the sofa on a Sunday afternoon. Nodding off was something only really *old* people did!

So I got out of bed. Time to complete my hand treatment, which meant going downstairs to find the sugar bowl and carry out the exfoliating bit. Apparently, if you put a couple of teaspoons of sugar into the palm of one hand, then rub both hands together like you're washing with soap, then you'll gently slough away all the old skin and hard bits and make your hands doubly gorgeous.

Only, as I got to my bedroom door, I was confronted with problem number three: How do you open a closed door when your hands are covered in grease? Answer: a) with difficulty because you can't get a grip or b) you just make a mess and have to clear it up later. I went with b).

Luckily, everyone had gone to bed so I had some privacy in the kitchen as I grabbed the sugar bowl and did the exfoliating bit. It was weird—a bit gritty—but the oil and sugar had definitely made my skin feel softer. I wanted to rinse my hands and was presented with problem number four: Fiddling with the kitchen taps when you've got oil and sugar all over you is not easy. Honestly! It was a good job the treatment did make my hands feel great because all the cleaning up I had to do after it was just dead boring. I was completely knackered by the time I finally got to bed. Though I did have very soft hands.

Anna and I like going swimming on a Sunday morning because you don't get all those noisy kids who like to bomb each other and jump into the water without looking (and who usually bomb *you* instead!). They tend to turn up with their blobby mums and dads at about the time Anna and I have packed in the swim and are heading for a double mocha in the café.

I made Anna laugh as I told her about the hand treatment I'd done the night before.

"But I reckon it's worth doing," I concluded. "Only I would recommend a bit of forward planning first— you know, with the door handles and stuff."

"I'll bear that in mind." Anna giggled. "So, soft hands *and* great hair—not bad going!"

It was true; the hair extensions disaster had given me a result. It was just a shame that I would never be able to afford to go back there for another cut . . .

"Right," Anna said, putting her mug down on the table purposefully. "I think that this week should be the week of the ear-piercing and tattoo."

"You do?" I said, slightly shocked. I mean, it was one thing thinking about having a tattoo. But *actually* having one was another thing entirely.

"Well, we've got some cash now, haven't we?" Anna said, looking at me expectantly.

"I suppose so," I agreed, gulping.

"That's settled then," Anna said. "We'll go to that tattoo parlor on the Winchford Road after school tomorrow. I heard someone say that they do piercing there as well."

And that was that.

Honestly, Anna was so excited at school the next day. She couldn't stop talking about the kind of earrings she was going to wear as soon as her ears were healed enough for her to change the original ones. She was clearly planning to wear a different pair every single day.

I wished that I could feel so relaxed about having a tattoo. I'd had my ears pierced when I was little, and didn't remember it hurting. My gran had taken me to get them done one year as an Easter present, much to my mum and dad's disgust. Gran didn't know they'd forbidden it until I was fourteen . . . but there wasn't much they could do about it once the earrings were in.

Now though, whenever I could get a word in edgeways, I tried to convince Anna that it wasn't such a good idea for me to get a tattoo. But she just kept saying, "Why not?"

I didn't want to admit that I was just plain terrified.

"Who's going to be able to see it on a normal day, anyway?" she said on the bus, later that afternoon. "If you have it on your back or your shoulder, most people won't see it."

"Then maybe there's no point in having one at all," I muttered. But Anna ignored me. She wasn't going to let me wimp out of this.

"I'm sure you have to be eighteen for a tattoo parlor to do it legally," I said, suddenly confident that I'd found a watertight way of getting out of it.

"Like the tattoo parlor's going to care," said Anna, jumping up and dinging on the bell for the driver to stop. "Come on—it's just over there!"

We'd both heard about the tattoo parlor on Winchford Road. It was called Skin Art and was painted a very dark blue. You could hardly see through the window because the shop name was painted in these swirly big rainbow letters across the glass. The door was set back so that a smaller side window could display photographs of tattoos they'd done.

"I can't go in there!" I said, frozen to the pavement outside.

Even Anna the Brave seemed to be feeling a bit apprehensive about going in.

"I'm sure it's okay," she said, not very convincingly. "Look—these tattoos are really good. I mean, look at that photo of the phoenix. It's cool."

"I suppose . . . but we don't know how clean it is in there, do we?" I protested.

"Well, why don't we go in and take a look round?" suggested Anna sensibly.

"But how will we get out again?" I said, panicking.

"Through the door?" Anna retorted, a little too sarcastically for my liking.

Before I had time to think of another protest, the door suddenly opened, and a customer came out.

"Here you go, girls," he said, holding the door open for us.

We went in. It would have been rude not to.

Chapter Twelve

"Afternoon—can I help?"

The voice was dark and gravelly and came from the corner of the room. The inside of the shop was small, and painted just as darkly as the outside. The walls were covered in photographs and drawings of tattoos. At the back of the shop, a curtain was drawn across a doorway. A very black curtain.

"Hello?" came the voice again.

"Oh, hello," I said, slightly startled as I finally focused on the owner of the voice. It was a woman—a very gothic-looking woman, with long jet-black hair. She was dressed all in black, with circles of black makeup around her eyes. She was scary. And she was surrounded by a stinky cloud of cigarette smoke.

"Come for a tattoo, girls?" she asked.

"No!" I squeaked at exactly the same time that Anna said, "Yes!"

I shot my best friend a death stare. She smiled back at me sweetly and started asking Scary Woman how much the tattoos cost.

"Something like this?" Anna asked, pointing toward something similar to the phoenix we'd seen in the window.

Scary Woman told us how much and we both gasped at the expense. Still, I thought, that gives me an even better excuse to get out of having it done.

"How much have you got?" she asked.

"We were thinking about something more along the lines of about fifteen pounds," Anna said.

We were?

"A Celtic symbol, then," the woman said, and pointed to a chart on the wall.

"Oh, I like those," Anna said.

I frowned. Who was having this tattoo—me or her?

"How about this one, Beth?"

I looked at the one she was pointing to on the chart. It was okay—in fact it was more than okay. I just wasn't that convinced that I wanted it indelibly marked on my shoulder for the rest of my life. I mean, what does an old lady look like with a tattoo? You know, when the skin has all gone wrinkly? Does the tattoo go wrinkly with it? In which case, how does anyone know what it was originally meant to be when it's all puckered up? Or, worse, droopy? And what happens if you get fat? Does the tattoo stretch with the flab? Or does it all break up? Yuck!

"It's okay," I said, my voice wavering a little.

"Tor could do it for you now," Scary Woman said. "Tor?" She called through the black curtain, and my stomach turned somersaults. This is going to hurt, my brain was telling me. Dad is going to go bonkers, it warned.

I felt sick. I wanted to run out of that dark little shop straight away. And when Tor came out from behind his curtain I *really* wanted to run! He was a giant of a man—and he was really hairy too. He had tattoos all over his arms and neck, even on one of his cheeks.

"Hello," he said, smiling to show off two gold teeth that matched his earrings.

Terrific, I thought. The man is a pirate. A pirate who does tattoos. I wondered if he had a parrot with him back there.

"Celtic symbol," Scary Woman said to Scary Hairy Man. "Sorry, girls, I don't know which one of you is having it?"

"Beth is!" Anna said swiftly.

Thanks, Anna, I thought, wishing the ground would swallow me up.

"Come in then, Beth, and we'll get going," Scary Hairy Man said, holding the curtain aside.

Anna shoved me from behind and we followed him into his darkened cave behind the curtain. That was when I began to freak. For a start, it was so dark in there I couldn't understand how he could possibly see what he was doing. And there was this kind of dentist's chair that he was expecting me to sit or lie on. ("Lie," Anna said helpfully. "You're having it on your shoulder.") Next to the dentist's chair was what looked like a drill.

"What's that?" I asked, panic making my voice shrill.

"That's what I do the tattoo with," Scary Hairy Man said, picking up the machine and switching it on. It made exactly the same whirry noise that a dentist's drill does.

Not on me, you don't, I thought, alarmed. That dentist's drill had a needle on the end of it. No way was I going to put up with that.

"Sorry," I said. "I think I'm going to be sick." I didn't really, but I said it so convincingly that I nearly did throw up. I jumped up and ran past Scary Hairy Man, past Scary Woman, and straight out of the shop. I didn't stop running until I got to the corner of Winchford Road.

Chapter Thirteen

It took a whole five minutes of our bus journey to school the next day and half a Twix before I forgave Anna for the tattoo "incident." We were just laughing about the hairy Tor when Frankie and her mates hopped on the bus. Anna groaned. As usual, Frankie looked around to check out who was going to be lucky enough to sit near her. But, instead of picking on a load of boys like she usually does (Frankie likes to be drooled over at every opportunity—and one boy is simply not enough), to our horror, she headed straight for me and Anna. Disaster.

"Well, hello there, Beth, Anna," Frankie said, smiling her most sucky-up smile and sitting down in the seat in front of us.

"Hello, Frankie," Anna said, coolly—as if it was perfectly normal to sit with her every morning. Then, equally calmly, "What do you want?"

"Want?" Frankie said, looking—or pretending to look—shocked. "Whatever do you mean, *want?* Really . . ."

Frankie turned to her followers who all looked at each other and tutted in support.

"I just thought how nice it would be to sit with you two," Frankie said. "So, how are you, Beth?"

"Fine, thanks," I said, wondering what on earth was going on. I mean, as far as Frankie is concerned, Anna and I are pretty much at the bottom of the food chain. We never normally even got to breathe the same air as Frankie, let alone to sit with her. Not that we were complaining.

"So you're not sore, then?" Frankie asked, just stopping herself touching my arm in "sympathy." Perhaps she was afraid that my H&M jacket wouldn't feel as nice as her designer label one.

"Sore?" I asked, genuinely puzzled. "What do you mean?"

"After yesterday, of course," Frankie said, smiling. "Why don't you show us?"

"Show you what?" Anna and I said, in unison.

"Your tattoo, of course," Frankie replied.

"What? How do you know about that?" I spluttered.

Was this girl some kind of psychic? Did she sit at home with a crystal ball, spying on what everyone else was doing? How did she know that I'd even been thinking of getting a tattoo?

"Yes," said Anna, leaning forward in her seat. "How *do* you know?"

"Well, I was told that the pair of you were seen going into the tattoo parlor in Winchford Road yesterday," Frankie said, looking pleased with herself. "And I was also told that Beth came rushing out afterwards, looking rather pale. So I assume it was her who had the tattoo, not you." She shot Anna a "stuff you" look. Anna didn't look too happy.

"So, Beth," Frankie continued, smugly. "Are you sore?"

Like she really cared. Her sympathy was totally fake.

"No—I'm fine, thanks," I said.

"Oh!" Frankie looked genuinely surprised. "But you did *have* a tattoo?"

"Yes," I said, emphatically. What was I doing? Why was I bothering to lie to Frankie, of all people?

"Show us!" Frankie demanded. "What's it of? Your boyfriend's name, maybe?"

It was typical of her to try to score one over on me. I'd surprised her by actually having a tattoo (even though I hadn't), so now she had to rub my face in the fact that, unlike her, I didn't have a boyfriend.

"Oh—that would just be tacky," Anna said, scoring a point of her own.

"Yes," I agreed hastily. "It's just a bird—on my shoulder."

Now why had I said that? If I'd just left it, then I wouldn't have got myself into the next embarrassing situation.

"On your shoulder!" Frankie crowed, delighted. "Show us! We'd love to see it."

The Frankie-ettes all started to wriggle in their seats with excitement, begging to see my tattoo.

"I'm not going to take my shirt off on the bus," I said quickly.

"As if," said Anna, like the true friend she is.

"But we want to see it," Frankie said, looking glee-fully at her gang, who smirked back at her. "Or perhaps you haven't *really* had a tattoo?" The ghastly girls gave a little giggle.

"Of course I have," I snapped. "I told you—a little bird on my shoulder. But I'm not going to show it to you on the bus."

There was an awkward silence, which was eventually broken by Frankie. "Well," she said. "I expect we'll see it in PE this afternoon, anyway."

Then she turned back to her friends with a knowing look. Anna and I exchanged a worried glance, and sat in silence for the rest of the journey.

At morning break, we had an emergency conflab. What was I going to do? Frankie was bound to notice there was no tattoo in sight during PE and then she'd never let me live it down.

Suddenly, Anna had a brainwave.

"I know where we can get you a tattoo!"

I looked at her in horror—she wasn't *really* expecting me to have another go, was she?

"Don't look at me like that, Beth! I don't mean a REAL one . . . We can go to the chemist's at lunchtime and pick up a temporary tattoo—they're pretty good. If you don't let Frankie get too close, I'm sure she won't notice it's not real."

Brilliant! What would I do without Anna?

So, in the girls' cloakroom a few hours later, Anna applied the temporary tattoo to my shoulder. It was a dove, the closest we could get to a phoenix, and nothing at all like a Celtic symbol—but at least it was a bird, like I'd told Frankie. Anna dribbled water over it to fix it in place.

"Whoa—that's cold!" I complained, fidgeting as the water began to run down my back and into my knickers.

"Remember: there's no gain without pain in the

world of beauty," Anna said, sounding just like a teacher. "And you are going to look SO gorgeous by the time you're sixteen that all this pain will be forgotten. There!" She stepped back to admire her handiwork.

"Well—what's it look like?" I said, straining to see my shoulder in the mirror by the basins. "Oh . . . not bad."

And it wasn't, either.

"How long do you think it will last?"

"Depends how much you scrub it in the shower," Anna said. "But I don't suppose you scrub your shoulders too much, do you? I mean—it's not like you've got loads of zits on your back like that girl Julie in the year above."

We giggled a bit, then felt rather shamefaced. Poor Julie. We'd seen her in the changing rooms once—she had so many spots on her back you wouldn't be able to fit a tattoo in, though you could probably play dot-to-dot. And she didn't have a single zit on her face. How weird is that?

"You know, I think I might ask you to do one of those on me," Anna said, as she threw the empty tattoo packet in the bin.

"Any time," I said. "Now—are you ready for PE?"

"Definitely!" Anna replied, smirking. "I wouldn't miss seeing Frankie's face for anything—even double netball!"

⑨

With Anna's help, I managed to only give a small flash of my tattoo to Frankie in the changing room. Just enough for her to see it, but not enough for her to realize that it wasn't the real thing.

If we'd thought it through a bit more, we could've just put a plaster on my shoulder and said it was healing, but now I had the temporary tattoo, I didn't want to risk pulling it off. I was beginning to quite like it.

Frankie couldn't believe that I'd actually gone through with a tattoo. She was so stunned that she shut right up for at least five minutes. Though it wasn't long before she was back boring everyone to death with news about a session she was due to have with a photographer "to get my modeling portfolio ready." Yawn, yawn. It was irritating, but I kept reminding myself that we were on our way to being gorgeous too. We just had to keep on working through that list . . .

Saturday came around fast, and before I knew it, there I was, back in my overall, lining up boxes and packets. I really got into my shelf stacking. I even got quite excited when they told me that I was going to have a 'supervised' session on the check-out later that afternoon. Sad or what? But I kept thinking about Jennifer Aniston's toned upper arms and the money I was saving up.

Now that I knew what I was doing, the time didn't seem to drag as much as it had the first week and it was lunchtime in a flash. As usual, I met up with Anna. We'd decided to bring sandwiches with us today.

"Think how much healthier they are," Anna said.

"And cheaper than chips," I said in agreement.

We sat on a bench near the recreation ground to eat, chatting away about our mornings and giggling.

We spent the rest of our lunch hour shopping. Mostly window shopping, except for a brief excursion into the chemist's.

"We need wax to de-fuzz our legs," Anna said.

"And fake tan to make them look gorgeous," I agreed.

So Anna bought the tan, and I grabbed some wax strips.

"I read in a magazine that strips are loads easier to use than hot wax," I said, as we left the check-out.

"Do you think your mum will let you sleep over at mine tonight?" Anna asked. "Then we could do the tans."

"I can ask," I grinned, liking the idea of an evening without my baby brother pestering me. "Why don't I give her a call now?"

Five minutes later it was sorted. I'd go home to get my stuff after work then head to Anna's for the night. And for a tanning transformation—hopefully!

Chapter Fourteen

I *like sleeping* over at Anna's house. Other people's mums just seem so much more laid-back than your own. I mean, my mum gets so stressy all the time and Anna's is like "Oh, okay!" about everything. I just don't understand it when Anna says her mum gets at her all the time. Her mum is chilled compared to mine.

Anyway, I whizzed home after work and grabbed my stuff before going round to Anna's.

"We're going to have a Ringa Pizza delivered," Anna's mum called down the stairs as I walked through the door. "Tell Joey what you want on yours and he'll ring up to order."

We watched some MTV (my mum and dad won't

even let us have Sky) while we ate the pizza. Then we left Joey in front of some film and went up to Anna's room.

"Going off to talk about lipstick and boys?" Joey teased, as we headed for the stairs.

"What makes you think we'd want to talk about you lot?" I joked.

"Yes, lipstick is far more interesting," Anna said, laughing.

Or, in this case, fake tan.

Up in Anna's room, I chose a CD and grabbed the tube of self-tanning lotion from Anna's bedside table. Total babe legs, here we come!

"It says we need to make sure we blend it in well on the ankles, knees, and elbows," I read. "And that we can't put our clothes back on for at least half an hour so that we avoid it coming off on the material."

"Good job we've got central heating these days!" Anna giggled. "And let's hope Joey doesn't burst in on us this time!"

I made a face—what a terrible thought. "Do you want to go first?" I asked.

In the end, we did our own arms and legs but each other's backs. The cream was a sort of fudge-brown color that made it easy to see when you hadn't rubbed it in properly. It stank a bit but we didn't care, as long as it made us look like we'd just spent a couple of weeks on the Costa del Sol.

"Right," said Anna, when she'd finished my back. "I reckon we can relax and read these magazines now."

Anna handed me one and sat down on her bed with the other.

"No!" I yelled. "You can't!"

"Can't what?" she asked.

"Sit down! The cream—if it comes off on clothes then it'll come off on your bedclothes too."

"Oh, for goodness' sake!" Anna sprang up from her bed double-quick. "My mum will kill me if I get brown streaks on my duvet cover—it's new. But we've got thirty minutes before we can sit down! What are we going to do?"

"Not a lot!" I said, and started to giggle. I mean, it *was* ridiculous. Here we both were, standing in our bras and knickers with our arms by our sides so we didn't get the cream on anything—and we had to stay like this for half an hour! The more I giggled, the more irritated Anna seemed to get. In the end she saw the funny side and the pair of us almost wet ourselves laughing.

"Don't make me want to go to the loo!" Anna wailed, clutching her stomach as tears rolled down her cheeks. "I'll probably leave a mark on the loo seat!"

At last we were able to get dressed, and we spent

the rest of the evening reading, gossiping, and listening to music. By the time we were ready to crash out, I still couldn't see any color change.

"Do you think this stuff really works?" I asked Anna.

"It better had," Anna exclaimed. "It cost enough!"

"But I can't see that much difference on my arms," I said, peering closely at the skin.

"It's the light," Anna said, confidently. "This artificial light doesn't show it up properly. Trust me—it'll be fab in the morning."

Amazingly, Anna was right. We both woke up looking healthy and glowing.

"Result!" I said, looking at myself in the full-length mirror that hung inside Anna's wardrobe door.

"Not bad," Anna said, admiring her own reflection as well as mine. "Not bad at all."

It wasn't until I was buttoning my jeans that I noticed a problem. "My hands! I thought I'd washed them enough, but they're brown!"

"Let's see," Anna said, peering at my mitts. "Yikes! They look like you've smoked fifty a day since you were a baby!"

It was true—my palms were dark yellow. They stank, too.

"Pooh!" I said, sniffing them. My hands were a dead giveaway. So much for my natural, golden tan.

"Come on," Anna said. "Don't worry about it. Let's go and get breakfast. Just keep your hands covered!"

Joey was already sitting at the kitchen table when we walked in.

"Well, hello!" he said, looking up from a mountain of toast.

"What's *your* problem?" Anna said, with the same tone of sisterly affection that I reserve for my brother.

"No problem," Joey said calmly, not reacting. Will would have yelled back at me childishly. But then he *was* particularly irritating. "I was just thinking how well you both look today. Kind of different. Have you dyed your hair or something? Or is it what they call beauty sleep?"

I blushed, but restrained myself from flicking my hair. I didn't want to ruin this moment by flashing my brown palms at Joey. Except for Greg's comment about my hair the other week, I'd never been paid a compliment by a boy. Nor by many other people, come to think of it!

"We haven't dyed our hair," I said.

"Well, whatever it is, you're looking good," Joey said, smiling at me.

"Haven't you got somewhere to go?" Anna said impatiently.

Joey looked at his watch. "As a matter of fact, I have," he said. "I'll catch you later. Nice to see you again, Beth."

"Thank God *he's* out of the way." Anna sighed grumpily. "What a pain. Now, one piece of toast or two, Beth?"

I pulled myself away from the sight of Joey's retreating back and smiled guiltily. "Er—one's fine, thanks, Anna."

What would my best mate think if I told her that I actually *liked* her brother? And that I was just trying to work out exactly how much . . . ?

Chapter Fifteen

"*It was just* AMAZING!"

It was Monday morning and Frankie was holding court as Anna and I arrived in the classroom. We slunk to our usual table at the back of the room. The Frankie-ettes were gathered adoringly round Frankie, clearly enchanted by her every word. It was enough to make you puke even *before* you heard what Frankie was talking about.

"Luciano says that I have the look of the century," Frankie simpered. "He says the camera adores me and that a *Vogue* cover is only around the corner."

"I suppose," Anna hissed, rolling her eyes, "we should be grateful we missed the first bus and didn't have to listen to this garbage all the way here."

I stifled a giggle and pretended to flick through my study diary. I wanted to hear all about Frankie's photo-shoot with the "world-famous Luciano." Only, I didn't want to *look* as if I was listening. Anna just slumped over the desk and closed her eyes.

"My booker at the agency says that the contact sheets should be with me by the time I get home tonight," Frankie continued. "I got to wear all sorts of outfits—casual, evening wear, sporty stuff, bikinis . . . all sorts."

"I bet you looked fantastic in them," sighed one of the Frankie-ettes dreamily.

"Yes," sucked another. "I can't wait to see them."

"Good grief," Anna whispered, sitting back up in her seat as Miss Anstey came in to take the register. "Her head's so big I'm surprised Luciano managed to fit it in the frame."

The next day, Frankie was positively buzzing with pleasure at her contact sheets.

"My booker is going to choose the best ones to go in my portfolio," Frankie explained to the entire bus. Even the driver kept turning round every time she stopped at a bus stop.

"They're amazing!" crooned a fan.

"Gorgeous!" adored another.

"Hideous!" yelled one of the boys at the back.

And every boy on the bus laughed hysterically as if

this was the joke of the century. Normally, I would have cringed at something so completely childish. But there was something really pleasing about the way it completely shut Frankie and her gang up. Made her blush with embarrassment, even. And return to earth with an unhealthy bump.

I looked at Anna. Anna looked at me.

"God," my best mate said. "I *really* wish I'd just said that!"

"So," Anna said on Friday, after lunch, "I thought we could do the waxing tonight. It's next on the list. Okay if I come round to yours?"

"I suppose so," I replied, though I was secretly sorry not to have the chance of seeing Joey. "Do you think it's going to hurt?"

"Not much," Anna said. "Anyway . . ."

"No pain without gain!" we said in unison, and laughed.

We went straight back to mine after school.

"Hello, girls," Mum said, as we walked into the house. "Fancy a drink?"

"Thanks, Mrs. Clarkson," Anna said, rather too "Little Miss Perfect" for my liking. "That would be great."

"So, tell me what you did at school today." Mum beamed and put the kettle on.

"Not much," I said.

"Loads, really," Anna said, as if she'd been in a parallel universe to me all day. What was she on about? We'd only been to school, not a trip to Paris. I hardly said anything as Anna told Mum everything we'd done at school in minute detail. She practically told her when we'd gone to the loo.

"Do you mind if we take our coffee up to Beth's room, Mrs. Clarkson?" Anna smiled. "Only, we've got quite a lot of project work we want to get out of the way before tomorrow."

"Of course, girls," my mother purred. "Here, take some biscuits with you. They should keep you going."

"Do you mind, Mrs. Clarkson? Thanks, Mrs. Clarkson. Project work, Mrs. Clarkson!" I mimicked in the safety of my bedroom. "Creep! What was that all about?"

"Privacy." Anna winked. "We tell your mum that we're going to be working dead hard and she's so thrilled that she leaves us alone and tells your baby brother that he can watch a whole load of tosh on telly that he wouldn't normally be allowed to, just to keep him out of our way."

I had to hand it to Anna—she'd got it all worked out.

"So," Anna said, snapping into action. "Where are those wax strips, then?"

"Here." I slipped the box out from its hiding place under my bed.

"Now, I read in a magazine that you should use talcum powder before you wax," Anna said. "Don't ask me why, but apparently it lessens the pain."

"Pain?" I said, panic in my voice. "What *kind* of pain? How *much* pain?"

"How would I know?" Anna said, giving me one of her looks. "I've never waxed my legs before, have I?"

"I'll get some talcum powder from the bathroom," I said, butterflies beginning to rise in my stomach. I hadn't felt like this since my piano exam.

Back in my room, Anna was sitting on the bed, her tights removed and legs ready for action.

"Here," I said, handing her the powder. "You can go first, seeing as you're ready."

"Thanks." Anna poured a massive pile of talcum powder into the palm of her hand and slathered it all over her lower legs.

"Okay." I pulled the instruction leaflet out of the box. "Erm . . . it says you have to apply the strips in the direction of the hair growth, press firmly, and then, pressing one hand on the surrounding skin, rip the strip off in the opposite direction to the hair growth. Oh, and you have to pull it quickly. God, this sounds as complicated as an AS level!"

"How many hands do they think we've got?" Anna said, taking the instruction sheet from me to have a look herself. "Hey—why are all the pictures of someone removing their mustache?"

"No clue," I said, having removed my own tights and started to apply the talcum powder.

"And why are all these wax strips so small . . .?" Anna said, tipping the contents of the box onto my bed.

"Aren't they always like that?" I asked, never having seen a wax strip before in my life.

"Not according to the magazine I read," Anna said. "They're meant to be tons bigger than these."

Anna looked at the box and then at me. "Did you look at this before you bought it?" she asked.

"Yes, no—I was embarrassed," I confessed. "I just read what it said on the shelf and bought them. I didn't want the girl on the till to know what I was buying. She might have thought I had really horrible hairy legs."

"Like she gives a monkeys about hairy legs when she's got to sell zit cream to pimply boys?" Anna said, exasperated.

"Oh, gross!" I said. "Okay, okay! So what does it say on the box that I missed?"

"That these are *facial* wax strips, you drongo!" Anna exclaimed. "That's facial—as in hairy lips. *That's* why they're so small."

"Oh . . ." I was lost for words. How hopeless was I?

"Never mind," Anna said. "We can still have a go. Only I don't know if there are enough here for us both to do our legs."

"Shall we just do yours, then?" I asked hopefully, still remembering the word "pain."

Anna raised her eyebrows. "Oh, go on then, I'll go first . . ."

"Ouch!" I yelled. "You never told me it hurt that much!"

Anna must have been biting her tongue when I did her legs because she hadn't made anything like as much noise.

"Don't be such a wuss," Anna said, applying a second strip to my calf and giving it a yank. Perhaps this was her revenge.

"Eeee-yowwwch!" I screamed. "You're enjoying this, aren't you?"

"Shut up and let me get on with it," Anna said, ripping away.

"Haven't you finished yet?"

"I said, shut up and let me get on with it!"

Get her! Still, I didn't have much choice. In the end, I stuffed a pillow into my mouth to stifle my screams.

"There!" Anna said triumphantly, at last. "I've run out of strips—that's all I can do until you get some more."

"You never told me it hurt that much," I moaned, stroking my legs to soothe the sting.

"If I had, you wouldn't have let me do it." Anna grinned. "So, what do you think?"

She hitched her skirt up and flashed her legs. They were red, patchy and stripy.

"What do *you* think?" I said, not sure if she realized that she looked like she'd been scalded.

"I think I need to put some moisturizer on them to cool them down," Anna said, grabbing a bottle of body lotion from my dressing table. "Hey, that's better. Oh!"

"What?"

"My tan!"

"What about it?"

"You yanked some of it off with the wax strips!"

"I did not!" I retorted.

"So where's it gone?" Anna wanted to know.

I inspected her legs. "Oh." Not only were they patchy and sore but underneath the red blotches there were white stripes.

I inspected mine. "Oh . . ."

"This is a disaster!" Anna wailed. "Not only have we got red blotchy legs, but we've lost our fabby tans too!"

"At least you've got fuzz-free blotchy legs," I pointed out. "Mine are blotchy, stripy, and only partly fuzz-free!"

Chapter Sixteen

For the last few days I had braved the chilly mornings (and ignored my mother's nagging) and gone to school without tights. I mean, why have fantastic tanned legs and cover them up? Especially when Frankie couldn't keep her eyes off them. She'd asked us if we'd had a spray tan and I was gobsmacked when Anna instantly answered that we had! She is such a liar! But she said afterward she'd just wanted to shut Frankie up because she's such a know-it-all.

Now, though, after the de-fuzzing situation, I was back to wearing the thickest, darkest tights I could find. There was no way I wanted anyone, *especially* Frankie, to see the mess we'd made of our legs. Luckily, no one gave them a second glance. Although that may have been partly because Frankie was droning on and on about her portfolio again.

"You know," Anna said, as we sat as far away as possible from Frankie and the Frankie-ettes in the dining hall at lunchtime, "I almost wish that she had been whisked off to Milan or New York for some photo shoot. Then maybe we'd be spared this daily torture."

"But what if she landed a mega deal with someone? Then her face would haunt us from every bus!" I pointed out.

"True . . . ," Anna pondered. "But at least she wouldn't be *on* it with us! Listen, who cares about that big bonce, anyway?" She whisked a sheet of paper from her pocket. "Our list is way more important. I've only got a few weeks to go before my birthday, remember?"

Like I could forget? I was going to be sixteen soon as well.

Anna spread the sheet discreetly between our two trays and we looked at it.

"The hair's getting there and we've sorted the jobs," I said, loading my fork with coleslaw.

"We've failed miserably on the leg front, though," Anna pointed out.

"Don't mention that!" I said, rubbing my leg at the very thought of the pain that I had suffered from the waxing. "The nails are pretty much okay, though."

"True," Anna agreed. "I hope you're remembering to rub that cuticle cream in every night!"

"I most certainly am," I said smugly. "Look."

I showed off my nails. Since we'd been doing the things on our list, I really had taken care of my nails. In the past, I'd only bothered to cut them when I absolutely had to. Now I kept them a uniform length with a nail file, applied the cream every night, and even buffed them. In one of the millions of magazine articles that Anna and I had read since we'd started our sixteenth-birthday mission, there was this thing about your nails being "jewels, not tools." We'd laughed when we'd read it but now we'd begun to seriously believe it.

"We've failed miserably to date any boys—even Greg and Baz." I moaned.

"Ugh, give me a break, Beth!" Anna said, her face screwed up in disgust.

"I know," I replied. "Who wants to go out with those tossers, anyway?"

"Still," Anna pointed out, "We've only got a few weeks to find a date, get into our drop-dead gorgeous gear, and chill out down at Cheeky Pete's."

"Okay," I said. "So how are we going to go about that?" Anna thought for a moment. "Who says we have to wait to be asked out? Maybe we should ask some boys ourselves!"

"Oh no!" I protested. "Absolutely not! No way."

"Beth Clarkson, you are a lightweight!" Anna said.

"I am not!" I retorted, a blush developing on my cheeks. "It's just that . . . well . . . I've never been asked out by a boy before . . . and, well . . . I'd rather my first date wasn't one I've had to fix up myself."

Anna looked at me. Then she shrugged. "Well, I've never been asked out before either. So, well . . . maybe I know what you mean."

She sat there, looking thoughtful. "Come on," she said, at last, looking back at our list. "What's the next thing left to make us so fantastic that the local hunks won't be able to resist our charms?"

"Our figures," I said, pointing at that particular item on the list.

"Hmmm," Anna murmured. "Got your purse on you?"

"Like I'd leave it at home for my slimy brother to raid?"

"Well then," Anna said, smiling again. "We'll go to Gammons on our way home and buy ourselves stuff that's really nice!"

"Euurgh!" I protested.

"Well, to create something better than a chessboard, anyway." Anna smiled.

And with that, she folded up our definitive list of ways to be fabulous and put it in her pocket.

"Do you think we need to be measured?" I wondered, as we hopped off the bus later that afternoon, right outside the department store.

"Don't yours already fit?" Anna asked, steaming ahead.

"Well, yes, but maybe we could get measured to make sure we're maximizing our assets?" I said, smiling at my own joke.

"Oh, hark at you!" Anna said. "Come on—bras are on the first floor."

We headed up the escalator, which conveniently brought us out at the exact spot.

"Wow," I sighed. "Look at those!"

I walked toward a stand that had the most gorgeous lacy underwear on hangers.

"My mum would never come home with something like these for me," Anna said wistfully.

I knew what she meant. My mum's idea of a bra was a sensible white cotton thing with thick elastic straps. Something that clinched you in an iron grip and made whatever you had splat into your chest and pop out at the back. And as for the knickers she bought me— well, Bridget Jones eat your heart out.

"They're really gorgeous," Anna said again. "But there's not much to them, is there?"

"What?" Was Anna suddenly on a value-for-money mission? This wasn't like her at all.

"I mean," Anna explained, "they probably look great if you have assets in the first place. But if you haven't, they're not going to do much in that department."

"No." I could see what she meant. "Maybe we need something with a bit of padding?"

"Good idea," Anna said. "Come on—let's look over here."

We headed off. The only place Mum had ever taken me to buy underwear was Bhs. I couldn't imagine how embarrassing it would be to look round a place like this with her. But I loved all the stuff that I could see here. All the fantastic colors and fabrics. Some of the bras were still in their boxes and had pictures of girls looking sensational in the contents on the front. The labels claimed that some could make you bigger. Others reckoned they could push you up to near your chin. Some said they did both. It was confusing to know which effect we should be aiming for.

"There are changing rooms over there," Anna pointed out. "Why don't we choose a selection of bras and see which ones make us look the most fantastic?"

"Okay," I agreed.

We split up and headed off in different directions. I found a couple of really pretty bras that were just about affordable—even if you got the matching knickers. But as I searched, my thoughts were interrupted by Anna's voice.

"Beth! This is what we need! Look!"

She came rushing across the shop toward me, bra in hand, still on the hanger, but with something dangling from it. Before I could make out what it was, I saw something else. *Someone* else. Someone who made me want the earth to open up and suck me in.

"Hello, Anna! Hello, Beth!"

It was Mr. Dalton. Our geography teacher—with a woman we didn't recognize. And he was in the bra department, standing right in front of us . . .

Chapter Seventeen

In the total world humiliation stakes, this particular moment in my life rated quite high. I mean, meeting my mum—or even my dad—couldn't have been worse than meeting Mr. Dalton just as Anna was waving a bra in the air!

"Bye, Mr. Dalton!" I squeaked, grabbing Anna by the arm and propeling her toward the changing rooms. I moved so fast I could have qualified for the Olympics.

"What on earth was *he* doing here?" Anna asked, closing the curtain on the changing room behind us.

I sat on the bench in the little cubicle and placed the bras down next to me. "That was so embarrassing! Mr.

Dalton saw us with these! Do you think that was his wife?"

"Maybe she was his girlfriend!" Anna suggested. "Fancy Mr. Dalton hanging out in bra departments! Maybe he was buying something for himself!"

We both giggled helplessly. When she'd got her breath back, Anna said, "You've got to admit that he must have felt a bit of a twit seeing us too."

I laughed again. Our next geography lesson was going to be SO embarrassing.

"What's so special about that bra, anyway?" I asked.

"It's perfect," Anna said. "Look." She held it up on its little hanger to show me. "See this?" She pointed to a little plastic thing that looked a bit like a tiny balloon.

"What does that do?" I wanted to know.

"It pumps it up," Anna explained. "There are air pockets inside the bra. You pump them up to get the size you want!"

"But it's not going to look very glamorous having that stuck inside your T-shirt, is it?" I pointed out, touching the pump.

"No, you idiot!" Anna said. "Once you've pumped it up you unplug it!"

"Hey, that's brilliant! Fancy inventing that."

"Come on—let's try it!"

An hour later—well, there were a lot of decisions to be made!—we'd chosen our bras.

Anna went for the one with the pump and I chose one that did up at the front and let you decide how much you squished yourself together. Just right for someone like me who didn't quite have the nerve to have herself poking out of her T-shirt.

"You know, I'm going to have to hide this in my room," I confessed to Anna as we finally set off home.

"Me too," Anna said. "Mum will go ape if she sees this thing."

"I reckon mine will be jealous," I said.

"But your mum's okay—she looks pretty good for someone her age, doesn't she?"

"You think?" I'd never really thought about my mum looking particularly good before.

"I know!" Anna said. "Haven't you seen the way Mr. Portman looks at her at parent-teacher evenings?"

"Oh yuck—it makes my skin feel slimy!" I knew exactly what Anna meant. Mr. Portman is the music teacher at school and he always went all smiley when he talked to Mum. Disgusting or what!

"Listen, I'll see you tomorrow, Beth!" Anna smiled and patted me on the back to say good-bye. "I'm off to practice pumping!"

The week plodded on by. The countdown to the big sixteen had begun. We both managed to hide our bras and keep them from our mothers'—and brothers'!— prying eyes. One night we did a hot oil treatment on our hair. It really did seem to make a difference to how shiny it looked. And we did the leg waxing again too. It was still excruciatingly painful but at least this time we managed—*I* managed—to buy the bigger strips of wax so the job was over quicker. Plus we discovered that if you do your own legs, somehow it doesn't seem to hurt so much. It still hurts, just not quite so much.

We'd tried tanning again—this time *after* we'd waxed—and it had worked well. I read that if you scrubbed away all the dead skin from your legs— exfoliating—then the instant tan goes on smoother and more evenly and lasts longer. Anna found some soapy stuff in her mum's shower that did the job, and we used that on our legs, this time without Anna's mum noticing we'd nicked her stuff. They did feel dead smooth afterward, even if I say it myself. And the tan soaked up beautifully too.

By now, my tattoo had come off completely. There had been some last black bits from the outline that I'd had to scrub hard in the bath. It had hurt, but they came off. Anna and I decided that we'd do another tattoo the night before our hot date.

Hot date. That was a laugh. It was too late now for Anna's birthday, which was only a few days away. So we were just going to have to sort it for my birthday. The problem was, we still hadn't managed to find anyone to go on the hot date with us . . .

"So, does it feel any different?" I asked Anna on the morning of her sixteenth birthday. I really hoped it did—because I wanted to feel different when it was my turn.

"I *think* so," Anna said, not sounding entirely convinced.

"How?"

"Well—I've got loads of presents for a start! And, well, it's hard to explain. It's just a kind of feeling. I'm old enough to leave school, get a job . . ."

"And get married," I added.

"Exactly—I don't think I can be called a kid anymore."

I'd given Anna a really gorgeous set of bangles for her birthday. She'd loved them as much as I'd hoped and put them on straight away. Unfortunately, Miss Anstey spotted them and told her to take them off. It was so not fair having to be at school on your birthday.

We did celebrate a bit that night. Anna's special birthday supper. Only my mum was way out of order and wouldn't let me sleep over "because it's a school night." It was still a really good evening—Anna's mum is a brill cook. Joey was there (and he kept telling these really funny jokes that made even Anna laugh). It was *so* embarrassing when my mum turned up to collect me like I was still a little kid.

118

"I've decided that I'm going to get my ears pierced tomorrow," Anna stated on Friday. "With some of the money I got for my birthday."

"Where are you going to have them done?" I asked.

"In that beauty salon next to the hairdresser's."

"Will they do them at lunchtime, then?"

"I think so," Anna said. "Well, I hope so, anyway. Will you come with me? I don't think I'm brave enough to go in on my own."

"You what?" I asked, not quite believing that Anna was feeling a bit nervous about having her ears pierced. That's ears pierced, not a tattoo with a whizzing scary drill like she'd tried to make me have. "Are you admitting that you're feeling a bit of a wimp, then?"

"Not a wimp, no," Anna said, avoiding my eye. "I'm just not very good with needles."

"But having your ears pierced is so easy," I said. "It's just a quick click and the earrings are in. Simple."

Anna winced as I said the word "click." "Are you going to come with me or not?"

"Sure I'll come with you," I said. "And I'll hold your hand the whole time if you want."

"Thanks," Anna said gratefully. "Only make sure you don't laugh at me."

"As if," I said, smirking.

At lunchtime the next day (I'd done shelf stacking all morning and was going to be on the check-out all afternoon) I couldn't work out if Anna's face was white or slightly yellow. She usually chats away, telling me about her morning at the salon. Only this time she was pretty much silent.

We were standing outside the beauty salon.

"Maybe I can get away with not having them done," Anna said suddenly. "I mean, there are some really good clip-on earrings nowadays, aren't there?"

"But you can't wear them in the swimming pool," I said. "And they might fall off when you're dancing at Cheeky Pete's. Or drop into your plate of food."

"Oh shut up!" Anna said. "Actually, I think I might be getting the flu. Probably not a good idea to get your ears done when you've got the flu."

"Stop being so pathetic, Anna," I said. "Come on, we're going in."

Once inside, Anna was too embarrassed to protest too loudly.

"She wants her ears pierced," I explained to the receptionist.

"Choose the ones you want from this chart and then we'll get someone to come along and do them."

"These look cool, Anna," I said, pointing to a pair with little diamonds in the middle.

"They're okay," she said, her lips pinched.

"Just okay or do you actually like them?" I asked.

I'd never seen Anna like this before. She'd been fine with the leg waxing. I was amazed.

"I like them—I'm just not sure I like the idea of them in my ears."

"She'll have those," I said to the girl. "Don't worry—she'll be fine."

Ten minutes later, after two tiny clicks, Anna had pretty little diamanté earrings in her ears. She'd also broken out into a cold sweat and was sitting, stunned, in her chair. I sorted out the money for her and paid, then grabbed her by the arm and dragged her to the chip shop. I figured that if Anna had some food inside her, she wouldn't go and faint on me.

It seemed to work and after a while Anna even confessed that she quite liked the earrings, as she stared at her reflection in the chip shop window.

"But they hurt!" she wailed, touching her ears.

"Leave them alone!" I snapped. "You've got to do what the girl said and make sure you keep the piercings clean or they'll go septic and then they really *will* hurt."

"Okay, okay," Anna said. "But they're throbbing!"

"They'll stop doing that soon," I advised her. "You'll be so busy back at the hairdresser's you won't have time to think about them."

"I hope you're right. Mum is going to go ape when she finds out about this. She's always said I should wait until I'm eighteen to get my ears pierced."

"Oh well," I said, "it's too late now. You'll just have to hide them with your hair. For the next two years!"

Chapter Eighteen

Anna managed to keep her hair drooping down over her ears for the next few days without her mum or dad finding out. She told her brother but he said they looked cool and swore he wouldn't tell. Would my brother do something as decent as that? As if!

But Anna couldn't stop fiddling with her ears at school. She did it all the time—I could see her during lessons. She said it was because they itched but I reckoned they itched *because* she kept twiddling with them.

Halfway through the next week, Anna met me at the bus stop one morning and said her earrings were throbbing again.

"Look," she said, pulling her hair back. "Do you think they're okay?"

I sucked in my breath. "Like no way!" I said. "Gross!" Anna's earlobes were red and swollen and the little diamanté studs were kind of sunk in the middle of them.

"Oh, thanks a bunch," Anna said, flicking her hair back down to cover them up.

"Sorry, Anna," I sympathized. "But have you been cleaning them properly every day?"

"Yes, sort of," she said, not looking me in the eye.

"So you haven't?"

"Well—touching the back of them with that antiseptic lotion makes me feel a bit sick."

"But poking them with your fingers all day doesn't?"

"Do you think I should do something about them?" Anna looked worried.

"I think you should go and see the school nurse as soon as we get to school," I said. "Don't worry, I'll come with you."

"Thanks, Beth—you're a mate."

"Well, I've seen worse," the nurse said, as she inspected Anna's earlobes with her surgical gloves on. "I don't think your ears are going to drop off—at least not this week."

She looked at Anna's shocked face and said, "It's just a joke! But seriously, you really *do* have to make sure that you clean them at least once a day—or you'll have to have the earrings removed and may be left with scar tissue."

She sorted Anna out and told her to come back at the end of the week.

"See—it's not so bad," I said as we came out of the nurse's room.

"Been to see the nurse then, have you?" It was Greg. He was standing outside in the corridor with a sniggery grin on his face. Baz was next to him, laughing.

"Nothing too serious, thanks," I said sarkily. "What about you two?"

"There's nothing wrong with *us*!" Baz said. "We know all about your problem."

"About what?" I hadn't a clue what he was on about. Why do boys always talk in riddles? At least, some did. Joey didn't.

"You know about it?" Anna said, startled.

Greg and Baz couldn't hide their laughter.

"Never mind, we won't tell many people!" Greg sniggered. And the pair of them walked off.

"Oh, that's just great," Anna spat dramatically. "Now the whole school is going to know about it."

"Well, it's only a pair of infected earlobes." I tried to comfort her. "It could be worse."

Almost as soon as I finished saying it, I saw the poster outside the nurse's room. The poster that informed the entire school that this morning's clinic with the nurse was the Personal Hygiene and Advice Clinic. No wonder there hadn't been a queue! Who in their right minds would be seen dead going in there? Except for me and Anna . . . in front of Baz and Greg. . . . Suddenly their riddle began to make a lot more sense.

"Actually, Anna, I think our problem just got a lot worse!"

It was awful. Dear Greg and Baz had kindly spread a rumor around the school that the pair of us had been to see the nurse. Half the school seemed to think that we had a massive problem with BO, and the rest appeared to have picked up on a rumor that we had a fungal foot disease that was highly contagious.

When we walked into the girls' loos at break, the place emptied within seconds. All the other girls were giggling and pinching their noses with their fingers, trying not to breathe. I opened my mouth to try and say something to the last girl as she left, but nothing came out. I simply didn't know what to say. Then I panicked.

"Do you think we really do smell?" I asked Anna, trying to tuck my nose under my arm and inhaling.

"Of course we do not smell!" Anna replied stropily.

"Oh, excuse me!"

Frankie and the Frankie-ettes were marching in convoy into the loo. As soon as Frankie, who was, of course, at the front, saw us, she turned up her nose as if a skunk had just visited and began to turn herself round, as if to exit.

"What's your problem?" Anna bellowed at her.

"The problem is hardly mine," Frankie said in her

126

most superior voice. 'The problem—or should I say problems—are entirely yours, aren't they? You know, I do believe that it is possible to have an operation if the sweating is uncontrollable."

"You what?" I said. "Which one of us do you think has got this problem? It certainly isn't me!"

"Nor me!" Anna added. "If you really want to know what's wrong, it's these!"

Anna pulled her hair back and displayed her red earlobes to the entire cloakroom.

Frankie stepped back and opened her mouth as if to say something. Only, for once, she was speechless. She closed her mouth again and then opened it once more. Still no words.

"Practicing to be a fish, Frankie?" I said. The girl had the grace to blush. But she still didn't say anything.

"Excuse me, I've got to go." I steamed my way through the Frankie-ettes and out into the corridor. Straight into Greg and Baz.

"Oh, it's you two!" Anna was only a step behind me, and she couldn't hide her anger. Not that I think she wanted to. "So, what is it you've decided? Have I got a BO problem or a gross fungus?"

Greg and Baz looked nervous. Their usual too-cool-to-drool expression disappeared. They looked uncomfortable. Suddenly the school hotties looked like a pair of plonkers. Again.

"Well, come on! Tell me!" Anna wasn't giving up.

"We saw you coming out of the clinic—that's all," Greg said, cringing.

"And you told everyone in school that one of us had hygiene problems—or something?" I wasn't going to let Anna have to sort this on her own. Apart from anything else, I was part of the rumor.

"We only mentioned it to Tozer," Baz said, rather pathetically.

"Who happened to mention it to the world!" Anna said. "Well—perhaps you'd just like to tell everyone that you made a mistake. The only thing that's wrong with me is my ears! Look!"

She pulled her hair up high, and twirled round to show the gathering crowd in the corridor.

The spectators seemed to be enjoying seeing Anna make planks out of Greg and Baz.

"Is there a problem here?"

It was Mr. Dodwell, the deputy head. He was really young and quite cute-looking and most of the girls in school had had a crush on him at some time or another.

"Not anymore there's not, Mr. Dodwell," I said.

And Anna and I walked off, heads held high. Anna even tucked her hair behind her ears to make sure that everyone saw them.

Anna and I were still fuming at lunchtime. But after the little scene at break it did seem that the rumor

128

about the sexual health clinic had been completely flattened. We noticed that Greg and Baz sat well away from us in the dining hall.

"And to think that we wanted to go out with them!" I said.

"Yuck!"

"Bit of a problem, though," I pointed out.

"Why?"

"We forgot to find a couple of replacements for them. Who are we going to try and date now?" I wailed. We were running out of time.

"Tony and Ed?" Anna pondered.

They were in our year and in the football squad. They were okay but a bit pimply.

"I don't think they look old enough to get into Cheeky Pete's," I said.

Anna sat in silence for a while. Then she said, "I'm beginning to think this whole thing has been a waste of time."

I didn't know what to say. She was right. It was a minging situation.

On Saturday, Anna and I decided that we would wear our new bras to work to try them out. I was quite pleased with mine and had begun to think that I might save up to buy another one. I met up with Anna at lunchtime. I'd bought us some salad from the supermarket and we headed to our favorite bench by the recreation ground to eat it. We were only a few meters down the pavement when Anna tripped, just managing not to drop her lunch as she bumped into a lamppost.

"You okay?" I asked.

"Fine—it's just these heels."

Anna and I had vowed to wear our bargain high heels whenever we could. We'd got quite good at walking in them—or so we'd thought. Only problem was that I couldn't really get away with them in the supermarket.

We finally made it to the bench and started to catch up on the morning's work gossip and plot our weekend. As we sat and chatted, I suddenly realized that I could hear an odd noise.

"What's that?" I asked. "Can you hear it?"

"Oh, yeah—that hissing sound?"

"Is there a bike near here?" I wondered, looking around. The noise sounded just like a tire deflating. But there was no bike to be seen.

"Oh my God—do you think it's a snake?" Anna jumped up on the bench, panicking.

"There can't be snakes around here, can there?" I jumped up too. We could still hear the hissing.

"What is it?" Anna said. "It's really close. Like it's right on top of us."

We looked up. Of course there wasn't anything above us.

"Have we sat on something?"

"Like what?" Anna asked. "Hey—it's stopped."

We both listened in silence. She was right. We climbed down from the bench and sat back down. Fortunately, no one had seen us.

"Weird," I said, carrying on with my lunch.

"Oh!" Anna looked down at her jumper.

"Spilled something? Here." I offered Anna a tissue.

"No thanks," Anna said mournfully. "I don't think that's going to help—unless I stuff it down my bra."

"Sorry?"

"The hissing noise was my bra! All the air has come out of one side!"

I looked at Anna. She looked lopsided, with one big boob and one that wasn't. I tried not to laugh.

"What's the world got against me this week?" she demanded. "I thought being sixteen was going to make a difference."

I giggled. "Well, at least it didn't happen at work," I said.

Anna laughed. "While I was washing someone's hair! Imagine!"

"It must have been when you tripped over," I suggested. "You must have knocked the valve thing."

Anna suddenly stopped laughing. "But what am I going to do this afternoon?" she wailed. "I can't go back to the salon like this!"

Chapter Nineteen

Fortunately, Anna's bra hadn't broken completely. There was a kind of plug thing on the valve that had been knocked out of place. Once she'd got home she repumped and replugged it and was able to have boobs again. But she'd had to stuff one side of the bra with loo roll for the rest of the day at work.

"We've still got a problem," I sighed as I lay back on my bed that night, having persuaded my mum to let Anna stay. "I mean, how are we going to find ourselves dates for next weekend?"

Next weekend was the one we'd set for our big night out at Cheeky Pete's. We'd sorted the hair, the nails, the boobs, the legs, the shoes, and the tattoos. We'd even got jobs and kind of worked out the ear-piercing situation. But we *hadn't* sorted the boys, which is where our sophisticated night at the club fell apart.

In two weeks' time, I was going to be sixteen. Anna already was. This year I'd persuaded my mum that a night out at the cinema with my baby brother in tow was not my idea of sixteen-year-old fun. So she'd agreed that I could go to the Italian on the High Street with Anna, at her and Dad's expense. *Without* her and Dad, and without my slimy brother. Result.

This didn't make up, however, for the fact that neither Anna nor I had yet been on a date. We'd been through all the possible candidates at school and ruled them all out as disasters, even before a date.

"Oh, it's no use," I wailed. "Do you think Joey's got any mates we could flirt with?"

"Joey?" Anna said, as if she had a bad smell up her nose. "My brother Joey? Well, he's got mates but I've never really bothered to look at them. They usually just come in covered in mud from football and eat their way through the kitchen, while I ignore them. And, anyway, they're my brother's mates."

"It was just a thought," I said.

We lay there in silence, listening to the radio. After a while, Anna shot upright and said, "Why do we need boys to get into Cheeky Pete's? We don't! We can go anyway! All we've got to do is get glammed up. Easy!"

"What?"

"If Frankie's done it, then so can we!"

"Oh—and how are we going to get all dolled up without our parents noticing?" I asked.

"Easy peasy lemon squeezy! My mum and dad are going out next Saturday—I know because it's my dad's work do and Mum's gone and bought herself some new dress for it. So we persuade your mum and dad that you're coming round to mine for the night—like tonight—only we get glammed up and go to Cheeky Pete's. My mum and dad will be back so late we'll easily get home before them. No worries. Sorted."

"Do you really think we could get away with it?"

"Sure!" Anna said.

And she was so confident about it that I believed her.

I worked on my mum and dad as soon as Anna went home the next day. I'd got my bedroom looking super clean, tidy, and organized and I even sucked up in the kitchen by helping to make lunch and making my dad a cup of tea when he came back from playing squash with our neighbor. It worked a treat. I was going to Anna's next Saturday night. As for Anna's parents, they, apparently, were only too pleased that Anna was going to have my company while they were out partying.

So we spent every spare moment the next week pampering and preening ourselves. We checked out the leg-fuzz situation, exfoliated, and planned to tan on Thursday—after all, we didn't want to fade too early, did we? We did more hair treatments to build up the super shine we'd cultivated. Even Anna's ears returned to normal and she braved telling her mum about them. She went bonkers at first but apparently Joey won her round by telling her that at least she'd been responsible and had them done in a proper place, rather than got me to do them with a needle. Anna just didn't realize how lucky she was in the brother department.

For Anna's birthday, her gran had given her this wicked eyebrow-and-lash kit. It had these heated eyelash curlers that you used before you put on the mega-curl mascara. Then you had different eyebrow shapes to choose from; templates shaped like famous pop stars' eyebrows. There was the Britney Brow, the Kylie Krowner, and the Christina Curl. The idea was that you chose the shape you wanted your eyebrows to look like and held it over your own eyebrow. Then you drew the shape of the template with a special eyebrow pencil and plucked any of the hairs that didn't fall inside the shape. Any bald patches inside the shape you just shaded in with the pencil. Easy. So one night after we'd done our homework, Anna and I had a go at it. Anna chose Kylie and I wanted Britney. We did each other's—and I'm telling you, someone else plucking your eyebrows is loads more painful than plucking your own. But the results were worth it.

So, by the end of the week we thought we were looking pretty good. We'd perfected the instant tan and we looked cool. We'd chosen the outfits we were going to wear on Saturday. For me: my hipster jeans and a T-shirt that I'd customized with some sequins. Anna was going to lend me a really cool leather jacket that she'd been given for her birthday. She was going to wear these funky black trousers that she got for her birthday too and a slim-fitting sleeveless polo neck. Now all we needed were some new heels from the shop on the High Street . . .

We went there at lunchtime on Saturday. Even if we'd pooled all our money we wouldn't have been able to afford a single pair. Not even one shoe. So we went back along the High Street and trudged into all the other shoe shops. We were beginning to run out of time. That was when I spotted the strappy sandal things in the window of the shop where everyone bought their trainers and wellies.

"Now *those* are distinct possibilities!" I said, grabbing Anna by the arm and walking her in.

"Are you serious?" she said.

"Deadly—look." I triumphantly picked them up from the shelf. Okay, so they weren't real leather. But they were shiny and strappy and high—and there were three different styles so we wouldn't look like twins. We each tried a pair on. They fit. They looked cool.

"All we need are perfectly painted toenails and we'll swing it," I said.

"You know, Beth," Anna said, smiling at me, "you're really getting quite good at this, aren't you?"

I went straight back to Anna's from work that night so that we didn't waste a moment. First we showered, then we applied this glistening body moisturizer that made our skin shimmer – another of Anna's birthday presents. We dried each other's hair and used her mum's straighteners. Then, with our jeans on, we painted our toenails, feeling dead pleased that we'd thought of doing them *after* the jeans so we didn't smudge them. With our boob-enhancing bras on, we wriggled into our tops, so that we could do our makeup without smudging them, either. The makeup took forever—we even curled our eyelashes before we did the mascara. But the results were definitely worth it. The final touch was our fingernails. We waited ages for them to dry because we were terrified that we were going to ruin them.

"Come on," Anna said. "Let's go downstairs to watch Sky while they dry."

So there we were, sitting watching the telly, all glammed up, when Joey came home.

"Wow!" he said, looking genuinely pleased. "No need to go to so much trouble just for me."

"As if," Anna pouted.

"So, what are you two dressed up for then? Off to a party? Mum didn't mention it."

"We're going to Cheeky Pete's," Anna said.

I was horrified. If Joey knew, he'd probably try to stop us. You had to be eighteen to get in, after all, and Joey was bound to know that.

"Are you meeting someone there?" Joey asked.

"Yes," Anna said, at exactly the same time that I said, "No."

Joey laughed. "I'll take it that's a no, then."

Anna glared at him and said, "Don't tell Mum and Dad, will you? Or we'll be grounded and it's Beth's birthday next week and we're meant to be going out for it. Please?"

"It's okay," Joey smiled. "I won't tell if you don't. But are you going to be all right getting there on your own?"

"It's not that far, Joey."

"No—but I'd just like to make sure you get in okay. If you don't let me do that then I might be persuaded to blab on you."

Anna glared at him.

"Would you mind?" I asked, quite liking the idea of Joey making sure we got in.

"No worries," Joey said and gave me another smile. "By the way, I like your shoes."

Half an hour later (it took us that long because we couldn't walk too fast in our heels) we were standing on the other side of the road from Cheeky Pete's. The entrance was buzzing with people, and cabs and cars kept pulling up. There were these huge guys in smart black suits standing outside, staring at everyone, but saying nothing. Every now and then, they opened a door and let a group of people in.

"Who are the chunky blokes?" Anna asked.

"They're the bouncers," Joey said.

"Bouncers?" I replied. "What are they for?"

"To check that nobody too undesirable gets in," Joey stated. "Or anyone underage . . ."

"Oh," I said, suddenly feeling much more like my actual age than I'd looked in Anna's bedroom mirror.

"So, shall I escort you across?" Joey asked.

"No," Anna cut in quickly. "I think we'd just like to wait here a bit before we go in. You can go now, Joey—thanks."

Chapter Twenty

"I hadn't realized how scary some of the people at Cheeky Pete's would be," I whispered to Anna.

We were still rooted to the spot where Joey had left us.

"The way Frankie speaks about the place I thought it would be full of really cool guys," Anna said.

"Even the girls look a bit . . . well, hard," I said, looking at one particularly rough-looking girl who'd just stepped out of a taxi with her mates. They were giggling and squealing with laughter. All of them had long blonde hair. And all of them were wearing skirts so short that even I was embarrassed for them. They didn't seem that worried, though. Nor did the bouncers, who greeted them so enthusiastically that it looked like they knew them. I noticed one of them was *seriously* kissing a girl.

"Oh, gross," I said. "Did you see that?"

"He'd better not try that on me," Anna said, shivering at the thought.

We stood and watched some more. We didn't see anyone much more glamorous arrive at Cheeky Pete's. But then this car came down the road. You could hear it coming for ages because the bass of the car's sound system throbbed as it approached. To my horror, it pulled up in front of us. It was full of boys with really short hair, kind of Robbie style. Only without the looks.

"'Ello girls," said the boy in the front passenger seat. "Fancy coming into Pete's with us? We'll give you a good night out."

The three other blokes in the car sniggered.

"No thanks," I said, hoping that Anna, who I hadn't even looked at, would agree with me. These boys were mingers.

"Thanks anyway, but we're waiting for our boyfriends," Anna said, quick as a flash.

"Looks like you'll be waiting a long time, then," the driver said and the entire carload of them burst into fits of laughter before they drove off.

"Oh please—they were revolting," Anna said, looking at me.

"Do you still want to go in?" I asked her, uncertainly.

Anna looked at me, then said, "Not really, do you?

I mean, if the whole place is full of nerds like that then I can't see the point."

"Come on—let's go back to yours."

"Who's that?" Joey bounced out of the living room when he heard us close the front door. "Oh, it's you two! I thought for a moment that Mum and Dad were home early. What are you doing back here so soon?"

"Oh—we just didn't fancy it once you'd left," Anna explained. "We didn't feel like it."

Joey didn't say anything. But his expression said a lot. Then he said, "Shall I make you some coffee?"

"That'd be really nice, Joey," I said. "Here, I'll come and help you—only first I've just got to get these sandals off. They're killing me."

Joey was really sweet. He didn't rub our noses in it at all. He just made the coffee and ignored the fact that he had sussed we had chickened out of trying to get into the club when we were underage.

"Thanks, Joey," I said, when he handed me a mug. "I appreciate it."

"My pleasure," he replied, and gave me the cutest of smiles.

"How hopeless are we?" Anna wailed the next morning when we were lying in her bedroom, another cup of coffee in our hands, flicking through one of her mum's catalogs.

"We've wasted everything we've tried to achieve over the last few weeks," I agreed, grabbing the New Look catalog that was still in its plastic bag.

I opened it up and turned the pages, not concentrating very hard.

"Do you really think that Frankie *enjoys* going to that place?" Anna wondered.

"Do you think she actually goes there? Miss Precious?"

"Good point."

It seemed impossible to imagine Frankie and any of the Frankie-ettes with boys like the ones we'd seen the night before. Not their type at all.

We drank our coffee in silence, still glancing through the clothes and feeling depressed about how disastrous last night had been; the night we'd been waiting for with such anticipation. Suddenly my eye was caught by something very familiar. Horribly familiar.

"Oh my God!"

"What?" Anna asked.

"Well, take a look at that!" I plonked the catalog in front of Anna.

"Oh my God! It's her! It's Frankie!"

And there she was, three whole pages of her. Wearing seriously naff jeans and very ordinary T-shirts.

"So much for *Vogue*, then!" Anna laughed. "The little liar."

"Well," I replied. "To be fair, she never actually said she was *in Vogue*."

"No," said Anna. "But she didn't say she was in the New Look catalog, either!"

We both laughed again.

"Suddenly Monday morning at school seems so much more appealing . . ."

I giggled.

"Too right," agreed Anna. "Mustn't forget to put this in my rucksack." She dumped the catalog in her bag with a satisfactory thud. "Come on, let's get dressed and have breakfast."

Joey was down in the kitchen, getting himself ready for his Sunday-morning football. I hastily ran my fingers through my hair to neaten it up a bit. Why hadn't I put some mascara on? I wondered why I was so worried about what I looked like in front of him.

"Hi!" Joey smiled. He really did have a cute smile. "Feeling better?"

I smiled back—it seemed to be contagious. "Yes, thanks."

"You make the coffee and I'll make some toast," Anna said. "Mum and Dad up yet?"

"No," Joey said. "Not a peep—they didn't get back until nearly three."

"Wow!" Anna exclaimed.

"Want a top up?" I asked Joey, reaching for his cup, my fingers touching his as I did.

"Thanks," he said. "Hey, you two—fancy helping me out next Saturday?"

"Doing what?" Anna asked.

"It's the football club quiz night," Joey explained. "We could do with some brains on our team. I wondered if you wanted to join us?"

Anna looked at me and I shrugged. "Why not?" I said.

"Great!" Joey said. "It's at the club at eight."

At last! The great day of being sixteen arrived! I was sixteen, just like Anna. She and I went out to the Italian for our meal. It was cool. So were most of my presents—except perhaps the rather dodgy sparkly bubble bath my brother bought me. But Mum and Dad had given me a voucher to spend at Top Shop which made me feel a whole lot better about life. The only problem was, now that I worked on Saturdays, I'd have to wait until half term to spend it! But the important thing was that at last I was SIXTEEN! And the rest of the week at school suddenly seemed loads better.

On the Saturday, after work, I went back with Anna to get ready for the football club quiz. We didn't take nearly as long getting dressed up as we had the week before, but as we left Anna's bedroom, I realized I'd broken one of my nails right down to the stump.

"That's disgusting!" I wailed. "Just when all the others were looking so good!"

"Tell you what—why don't you put on some false ones?" Anna suggested. "I've got some in my drawer." She rummaged around and found them. "Here!"

They were quite long and a kind of fuchsia color.

"Don't you think they're a bit much for the football club?" I asked.

"Think *Footballers' Wives* and they're not!" Anna laughed. "Come on, I'll help you."

So we stuck them on and they fixed quite quickly.

"Ta da!" I said, waving my fingernails proudly.

"Come on—let's go win that quiz!"

It was a short walk to the clubhouse. I was surprised how many people were there: We had to push our way through the crowd, following Joey as he looked for his team over in the far corner.

"There he is!" Joey said, smiling at us. "Sam, this is my sister Anna and her friend Beth."

"Let me get some drinks," Sam said. "Cokes okay for everyone?"

"I'll help you," Joey said. "You girls sit here and keep our table."

"Hey, he's quite cool," Anna said, ogling Sam as he went. "Joey's kept him out of my sights!"

"He certainly is gorgeous," I replied. "So, where's the rest of the team?"

"Oh, it's just us," Anna said. "Teams of four: Sam, Joey, you, me."

"Oh," I said, surprised.

Before long, the boys were back and the quiz started. It was a real giggle. Joey was just so funny. And I noticed that Anna was flirting with Sam—who didn't seem to mind at all. When we didn't know the answers to questions, neither Sam nor Joey teased us. We didn't win, but we didn't do too badly and when it was over, we stayed and chatted a bit before going home.

"Fancy coming round for coffee?" Joey asked Sam.

"That sounds like a good idea to me," Sam said, helping Anna with her coat.

Anna was staring intently at him.

She fancies him, I thought. And he fancies her.

"You're coming back too, aren't you, Beth?" Joey asked.

I looked at my watch. "I'd love to but I'd really better get back."

"Oh," said Joey, looking disappointed.

"Tell you what, Joey," Anna suggested. "Why don't you walk Beth home and Sam and me will go back and get that coffee ready?"

"Good idea," Joey agreed quickly.

So that's what happened. I hugged Anna good-bye and then set off with Joey.

"It was a good evening, wasn't it?" Joey said.

"Really good fun."

"More fun than last week, then?"

"Much!" I laughed. "That was just awful."

"Cheeky Pete's isn't such a great place, you know," Joey confessed. "People make out it's really cool, but it's just a glorified pub. With a whole load of tossers in it."

I laughed again. "I know what you mean."

"I don't want you to get this wrong, Beth," Joey said. "It's not that you didn't look great last week— you know, with your makeup and those high heels and everything—but . . . well, you look great all the time, without all that stuff."

I was a bit surprised. I just looked at him and said nothing. I hate to admit it, but I think I blushed.

"I haven't offended you, have I?" Joey asked. "I mean, you looked really good last week—terrific even. But you look better the way you're dressed tonight. So does Anna."

"Thanks," I said. I was glad it was dark because my cheeks must have been scarlet.

We were almost at my gate when Joey said, "Beth, hold up. There's something in your hair."

"Oh, yuck—what?" I ran my fingers through my hair, panicking. "Is it an insect?"

"Keep still—here." Joey pulled something from my hair and held it up in the lamplight.

"What is it?" I looked. "Oh no!"

148

"I *think* it's one of your nails," Joey said, handing it to me. I thought I was going to die. "Like I said, you're lovely enough without them."

"Thanks," I replied, taking it quickly. "Well, night, Joey—and thanks for walking me home. I really enjoyed this evening."

"So did I," Joey said. "In fact, I was wondering if you'd come out with me again next Saturday."

"Is there another quiz?" I asked.

"No—I'd just like to go out with you on your own," Joey said.

He'd just asked me out on a date. I was sixteen *and* I'd just been asked out on a date. Hurrah!

A short while later, I was sitting on my bed, taking in what had happened, when my phone beeped. It was a text from Anna.

Sams askd me on d8!

So I'd been right about those two! I sent a text back.

Gr8! + iv gt 1 wiv JoE!

It looked like we'd managed the ten things after all. It might not have been *before* we were sixteen—but it was only *just* after!

About the Author

Caroline Plaisted worked in publishing for fourteen years before becoming a full-time writer. She has written for the BBC, Bloomsbury, and Kingfisher. She lives in Ashford near Kent with her two children, two dogs, and two cats.

Ella Mental

And the Good Sense Guide

a novel by
Amber Deckers

Ella (Mental) Watson is a rules girl,
always on hand to offer impeccable
advice. But when life gets complicated,
will the rules go out the window?

From Simon Pulse
Published by Simon & Schuster

truth or dare

By the bestselling author of the Mates, Dates series,

Cathy Hopkins

Meet Cat, Becca, Squidge, Mac, and Lia. These girls and guys are totally tight—and totally obsessed with the game of truth or dare . . . even when it reveals too much!

Every book is a different dare . . . and a fun new adventure.

Read them all:

White Lies and Barefaced Truths

The Princess of Pop

Teen Queens and Has-Beens

Starstruck

Double Dare

 Midsummer Meltdown

From Simon Pulse
Published by Simon & Schuster

The books that all your mates have been talking about!

Collect all the books in the bestselling series by

cathy Hopkins

Mates, Dates, and . . .

Inflatable Bras
Cosmic Kisses
Designer Divas
Sleepover Secrets
Sole Survivors
Mad Mistakes
Sequin Smiles
Tempting Trouble
Great Escapes
Chocolate Cheats
Diamond Destiny

Sizzling Summers

Only one book to go in this fab series!

"Bridget Jones as a Teen"
—Teen People

WANTED

Single Teen Reader in search of a FUN romantic comedy read!

How NOT to Spend Your Senior Year
BY CAMERON DOKEY

Royally Jacked
BY NIKI BURNHAM

Ripped at the Seams
BY NANCY KRULIK

Cupidity
BY CAROLINE GOODE

Spin Control
BY NIKI BURNHAM

South Beach Sizzle
BY SUZANNE WEYN
& DIANA GONZALEZ

She's Got the Beat
BY NANCY KRULIK

---

30 Guys in 30 Days
BY MICOL OSTOW

Animal Attraction
BY JAMIE PONTI

A Novel Idea
BY AIMEE FRIEDMAN

Scary Beautiful
BY NIKI BURNHAM

Getting to Third Date
BY KELLY McCLYMER

Dancing Queen
BY ERIN DOWNING

Major Crush
BY JENNIFER ECHOLS

Available from Simon Pulse Published by Simon & Schuster

Lightning Source UK Ltd.
Milton Keynes UK
UKOW031118210513

211006UK00007BB/139/P